W9-AGE-907

ALSO BY KATY KELLY

MELONHEAD

MELONHEAD

BY KATY KELLY

ILLUSTRATED BY GILLIAN JOHNSON

ORANGE COUNTY LIBRARY
146 A MADISON RD.
ORANGE, VA 22960
(540)-672-3811

DELACORTE PRESS

Published by Delacorte Press
an imprint of Random House Children's Books
a division of Random House, Inc.
New York

This is a work of fiction. Names, characters, places, and incidents either are the
product of the author's imagination or are used fictitiously. Any resemblance to actual
persons, living or dead, events, or locales is entirely coincidental.

Text copyright © 2009 by Katy Kelly

Illustrations copyright © 2009 by Gillian Johnson

All rights reserved.

Delacorte Press and colophon are registered trademarks of Random House, Inc.

www.randomhouse.com/kids

Educators and librarians, for a variety of teaching tools, visit us at
www.randomhouse.com/teachers

Library of Congress Cataloging-in-Publication Data
Kelly, Katy.
    Melonhead / Katy Kelly. — 1st ed.
        p. cm.
    Summary: In the Washington, D.C., neighborhood of Capitol Hill, Lucy Rose's friend Adam
"Melonhead" Melon, a budding inventor with a knack for getting into trouble, enters a science
contest that challenges students to recycle an older invention into a new invention.
    ISBN: 978-0-385-73409-7 (hc) — ISBN: 978-0-385-90426-1 (glb) —
    ISBN: 978-0-375-89192-2 (e-book)
    [1. Inventors—Fiction. 2. Washington (D.C.)—Fiction. 3. Humorous stories—Fiction.]
I. Title.
    PZ7.K29637Me 2009
    [Fic]—dc22
                                    2007046076

The text of this book is set in 14-point Goudy.

Printed in the United States of America

10 9 8 7 6 5 4 3 2 1

First Edition

Random House Children's Books supports the First Amendment and celebrates
the right to read.

For my five splendid nephews,
Tommy Rizzoli, Tom Kelly, Jack Kelly, Mickey Conroy, and Jimmy Conroy,
who, along with my brother, Michael, taught me the ways of boys

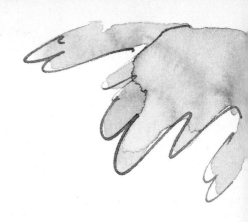

1

NOT MY BEST IDEA

Yesterday I was a regular ten-year-old boy. Today I'm the star of four Washington, D.C., TV stations. Channel 5 showed my picture with the words: *Tragedy Averted*. My friend Lucy Rose says averted is the same as avoided. I knew it would be. I have had a lot of aversions in my life.

This one started when I was climbing up Madam and Pop's magnolia tree with a rope in my teeth. It was for hoisting my best friend, Sam. Our plan was to get high enough to leap onto the breezeway roof that connects Madam and Pop's house to their carriage house. That's the same as a garage. We were going to lie on our stomachs and

CHANNEL 5

TRAGEDY AVERTED!

terrorize people down below by calling out, "We're watching you," in wavy voices and then make creepy "heh-heh-heh" sounds like we are deranged. We've done it before and it's hilarious. People can't figure out where the voices are coming from. Sometimes they talk to the air and say, "You're not scaring me," but we are. Believe me. Once a lady blamed a man who was doing nothing but trying to get to the corner before the light turned red.

I could have taken the tree-free route to the roof by going in their front door, cutting through the morning room, then racing up the back staircase, into the bathroom, and out the window. I'm allowed because I am one of Madam and Pop's good friends. I met Madam last year when I was in her tree box collecting good-smelling weeds for my deodorant-making experiment that was supposed to make me rich. I could tell that she was a friendly lady because she came rushing outside waving at me with both arms. I told her, "Don't worry. You don't have to pay me for pulling up this scraggly junk."

It was a big shock to me when she said she planted it on purpose. "Our yard is going to be on the Capitol Hill House and Garden Tour next week," she said. Then she told me everything there is to know about the plant scraps that were in my hands.

"I am sorry," I said. "I never heard there was a plant called lavender. And who would ever guess since it's mostly green? Not me."

By the time we finished reburying roots we were friends and she said, "Drop by and see us sometime, Adam."

"It's a deal," I said.

I keep that deal three or four times a day. A lot of times I go to get a snack or to visit Lucy Rose, who is their granddaughter. She sleeps at their house when her mom is working late. Other times I go to help Pop. He's Madam's husband and he has tons of chores. That's how come I know how to patch window screens and caulk sinks and pick about 1,000 apricots in only one day. It was when we were apricot picking on the breezeway roof that Pop said, "Feel free to climb out our bathroom window and wander around out here on the roof anytime."

"Thanks," I said. "But I'd rather go by tree."

"Anyone would," Pop said.

He and I think alike.

But yesterday Sam said, "Let's take the bathroom window shortcut to save time."

"It won't take me seventeen seconds to shimmy up the tree," I said. "I need to practice the improved climbing method I invented after the old method overstretched my ribs and Dr. Stroud had to tape them back together."

"Explain this new method," Sam said.

"Step One: I stand on your shoulders," I said. "Step Two: I throw my arms around the fattest branch."

"Cheese, Louise," Sam said. "Your new sneakers are poking ditches into my collarbones."

"So sorry, Mata Hari!" I said.

One of our habits is making up rhymes that are like "See you later, alligator." Only ours are ten times better.

"I like the old method better," Sam said.

"I'm almost up," I said. "I'm hooking my legs around the branch."

Flipping right-side up is the hardest part. Sliding down the branch is the most stomach scraping. The rest is E-Z P-Z.

"I've got one foot in the V of the tree and I'm starting to climb."

Only one leg went forward and the other one went backward. Right when I was thinking Goodbye My Sweet Life, my foot was stopped by a crooked hole that I never knew was there. Unluckily the hole swallowed my foot, whole. The only part of my high-top showing was a sliver of black. My toes were too

mashed to wiggle. "Get going, Melonhead," Sam hollered.

Melonhead is what I like to be called. Adam Melon is what my mom likes me to be called. My dad doesn't care what people call me because, for most of his childhood, his nickname was Pukie.

"I can't," I told Sam. "My size-four foot is stuck in a size-three hole."

"Quit horsing around," he said.

"I'm as serious as a D in deportment," I said.

Then he knew it was no joke. We both have trouble in the deportment department.

"I'm going for a grown-up," Sam hollered, and ran out of my sight.

"Make sure it's a good one," I shouted. Some grown-ups, like Mr. Pitt, the counselor at school, have a way of making things worse. Believe me, I know.

Being left was not the best feeling but it was the only way because Madam and Pop's house is on the corner so even though the breezeway and carriage house are on Fifth Street, their front door is on Constitution Avenue.

The next things I saw were two red and blue striped socks and two legs coming out of the upstairs bathroom window. They were attached to Pop. He walked across the roof and said, "Your foot has disappeared into a hole?"

"It's more like a short tunnel that has no exit," I said.

Down below, Sam was dragging Pop's ladder across the driveway. "Never fear, Paul Revere," he shouted. "I'm climbing to the rescue."

"One boy per tree," Pop said. "House rule."

Then he asked me: "Can you untie your shoe?"

"Nope," I said. "The laces are inside. They're tied tight and double-knotted."

"Double-knotted?" Pop said.

"I do that for safety," I told him.

"Of course," Pop said. "What happens when you try to pull your foot out?"

"It doesn't move," I said.

"I've got it!" Sam shouted. "Stuff butter around your ankle. Your foot will slide out."

"That's using the old bean," Pop said.

A minute later Madam was in the driveway, tying a short green bottle to one end of my rope. "Olive oil should work," she said.

"I married a genius," Pop said.

I reeled it up and poured. Then I pulled until my muscles felt shredded. "My leg is covered with slime," I yelled. "But the oil won't drip into my shoe."

"How is the rest of your body?" Pop asked.

"Fine," I said. "My shirt got most of the mangling."

I knew Madam was trying to lure my mind off my foot because her question was, "How's the view?"

"It's good," I said. "Miss Elsie is feeding pigeons off her porch. She's close so she looks like usual.

The Capitol dome looks miniature because it's five blocks away."

"Is the light on?" Sam yelled.

"Yep," I said.

Near the top of the Capitol dome, right under the statue, there is a white light. It stays on until the Congresspeople finish voting, even if it's midnight. Sometimes the Congressman who's my dad's boss is the one holding things up. When my mom and I want to know if my dad's coming home for dinner, we look out our back door. If the light's on we eat in the kitchen.

"Adam," Madam said, "I need to make a call. I'll be back in a bit."

One of Madam's talents is that when a problem happens, she stays relaxed.

I turned my head and some of my body to have a look at Fifth Street.

"Now I spy a blob of red hair," I yelled up to Pop. "It's Lucy Rose. She's with Jonique McBee and Gumbo."

Jonique is Lucy Rose's best friend. Gumbo is

Madam and Pop's gigantic black poodle. "Gumbo is wearing a fluffy pink ballet skirt," I said.

"That is tutu much," Pop said.

When Lucy Rose spotted me, her red cowgirl boots started hitting the sidewalk so fast it sounded like clapping. Jonique caught up quick. Gumbo got ahead of both of them. Running was making his tutu spin around his stomach.

"What on this earth is going on?" Lucy Rose yelled.

"Melonhead's foot got sucked into the tree," Sam said.

She put her hands on her hips and said, "For heavens to Pete's sake, Melonhead. Just give it the most tremendous yank."

"What do you think I have been doing?" I yelled. "It's like it's in cement."

"Is it fun being trapped?" Jonique asked me.

Actually, it was embarrassing but I told her, "Fun by the ton."

"Plus it's an experience," Lucy Rose said. "And you are one boy who is in love with experiences."

"I am not in love with anything," I said.

"Do you want Kleenex?" Jonique asked.

"No," I said. Jonique and her mom think Kleenex is the cure for everything.

"You guys go inside," I said. "I'll get unstuck soon."

"Don't be silly, Willie," Sam said. "YOU are where the action is."

I did not feel like rhyming.

"We don't mind waiting," Jonique said.

I did mind because people kept stopping to see what they were look-ing at and Lucy Rose was telling everybody the whole story and was being completely dramatic about it.

Mrs. Lee said, "I never heard of a

boy stuck in a tree. Only cats. And cats are not that smart."

A teenager said, "What a chucklehead."

I could feel my ears heating up. That happens when I'm a chucklehead. They turn red. Then pink creeps over my cheeks. Mr. Lee, who must have supersonic eyes, told his wife, "His face. It's like a tomato."

"He's like a cat and a tomato," she said.

Nobody, not even Sam, was telling about the trillions of times my foot didn't get trapped.

Pop was swishing the leaves over my head but I didn't look up. My eyes were stinging and my nose started to drip. I wiped them on my sleeve.

"It's awful to see what jealousy does to people," Pop whispered loud enough for me to hear.

"Who would be jealous of me?" I said.

"It takes courage to climb a tree," Pop said. "Not everyone has it. Some people have never climbed a tree in their lives."

"They never got stuck, either," I said.

"True," Pop said. "They also never got to see the world from a tree."

I was feeling better when, all of a sudden, it sounded like Capitol Hill was being invaded by howling hyenas. Everyone turned to look. I didn't. I just yelled, "Calm down, Mom!"

When I did look, there was my mother, running in high heels with her long black dress pulled up to her knees. Her party hair was lopsided.

"Your mom dressed up for this foot-freeing event," Pop said.

"She's supposed to be meeting my dad downtown at a dinner where people give money so the Congressman can buy bumper stickers that say Reelect Buddy Boyd," I said. "She is going to be unhappy about the situation my foot is in."

"She should thank you," Pop said. "I'd rather eat a thousand old socks than go to ONE of those dinners."

By then my mom was under the magnolia, looking up.

"You ARE in a tree!" she said.

"I am," I said.

"Really, Adam," she said, "this is too much. Come down this instant."

"I want to come down," I said. "It's my foot that doesn't."

My mom's cheeks drooped. "When I heard you were stuck I said, 'He CAN'T be because I have to be at the Mayflower Hotel by six o'clock.'"

"Go!" I said. "This is not the biggest deal."

"Nonsense," she said. "A boy needs his mother at a time like this."

Then came the horrible sound of air sucking.

"Please, Mom," I said. "Don't start breathing."

When my mom's in a panic she inhales and exhales super-fast.

Aunt Cindy says she started doing that the day I turned two and figured out how to open child-proof locks.

Aunt Cathy blames the speed-breathing on the time I escaped and pedaled my tricycle across East Capitol Street during rush hour.

My Aunt Traci says it started when Santa Claus asked me what I wanted and I said, "Dainjis, dainjis chemicals."

When my aunt told me that story, I told her, "I

was only three. Of course, I didn't know how to say 'dangerous.' "

My dad says that my mom only had sisters so she is unfamiliar with the ways of boys.

Luckily, this time the breathing didn't last. My mom pushed her hair off her face and yelled, "I'm coming to sit with you so you won't be scared."

"I'm not scared," I said.

"Of course you are," she said. "I'm scared out of my wits."

By then she was at the top of Pop's ladder standing on the step that says DO NOT STEP ON THIS STEP. Her silver high heels were wobbling but she turned and sat on the fat branch. When it bounced, she grabbed the air.

"Hold my hand for your comfort," she said.

That was the most embarrassing thing I could think of doing.

"Help is on the way," she said.

"Who?" I asked.

"Dad, of course," she said. "Who else would I call?"

No one else, that's who. My dad is great at grilling, treadmill walking, and picking out presents. But he is not a rescuer. Nobody taught him about lifesaving when he was a kid. Probably because most of the time, he was carsick.

"Neighbors are piling up under us," I said.

The annoying Ashley, who is in Mrs. Timony's class with me, was stomping on Madam's lavender and shrieking, "What if you have to pee?"

Until she said it, I didn't have to.

"Ashley," Lucy Rose said, "it is utterly rude to talk about pee in front of the public."

Ashley's answer was drowned out. A hook-and-ladder truck, three police cars, and one ambulance stopped in the middle of Fifth Street. I was about to ask, "What's the emergency?" Then I realized I was. They turned off the sirens but, since it was almost dark, the red and white whirling lights stayed on. A policeman put up orange triangles to detour the traffic and drivers started honking for no reason.

"This is one delightful hullabaloo," Lucy Rose said.

"Don't look, Harry," Mrs. Mannix said. Harry, who is her son that's in kindergarten, looked anyway.

"Does he get scared easily?" Mrs. Pecore asked.

"No," Mrs. Mannix said. "He gets ideas easily."

Next Mr. Neenobber stopped by. He was carrying his bagpipe and wearing his kilt that looks exactly like a skirt. "All that's needed to loosen the boy's foot is WD-40 and a stuffing spoon," he said.

Lucy Rose's mom tells everyone that a great thing about city living is meeting people who aren't like everybody else and Mr. Neenobber is not. Believe me.

"Thanks for that idea," a policewoman said. "But right now we're making room for the cherry picker."

All my embarrassment disappeared. "Man-o-man alive," I said. "This is the luckiest day I ever had."

"This is one of the more nerve-wracking I've ever had," my mom said.

"There are no cherries," Mr. Neenobber said. "That's a magnolia tree. It's altogether fruitless."

Nobody told him that cherry pickers are machines that rise up in the air so firemen can rescue people stuck in high places.

"Can you get out of the tree, Mrs. Melon?" a bald policeman asked.

"Yes," my mom said. But she kept sitting.

"I can throw you over my shoulder and carry you down if you like," a fireman said.

"That's the offer of a lifetime!" I said. "Go for it, Mom!"

Instead she dug her red beauty shop fingernails into the bark and lowered herself. Her high heels flew off. One landed in the birdbath. But her feet landed on the Do Not Step step. The best part is that the whole time her eyes were closed.

"Don't worry, Mrs. Melon," Sam yelled. "If you fall, the fireman will catch you by your butt."

My mom thinks talking about butts is vulgar. I think it's hilarious. Once, I told my dad that I am unfamiliar with the ways of ladies.

2

A DARK AND STORMY NIGHT

An orange and black Diamond taxi stopped by the detour and my dad jumped out in time to see my mom wobbling down the ladder.

"Hey there, sport," he yelled. "How's it going?"

"I'm fine," I screamed. "Great, actually."

"I'm sure you are," he said, and ran to help guide my mom down.

At the same time the cherry picker pulled in the driveway and a fireman jumped into the picker's white box and yelled: "UP!" The box stopped one inch from crashing dead into my free leg.

"Do I get to ride in that?" I asked.

"As soon as we get your foot out," he said.

"Outstanding," I said. "I'm Melonhead."

"Good name," he said. "I'm Gus Lynch."

"Thanks for coming, Mr. Lynch," I said.

"Call me Gus," he said. "When two men are partners in a rescue operation, there's no need to go all formal."

"I like talking man to man," I said.

"Me too," Gus said. "I've got a house full of daughters. They don't leave me much room in a conversation."

"I've got a mom," I said, and for a second I felt like I was going to cry.

"I saw her," Gus said.

"She's a worrier," I told him.

"She loves you," Gus said.

"I know," I said.

"My wife tries to get me to wear sports jackets," he said.

"She probably loves you, too," I said.

"Sometimes it's not easy to be loved," he said. Then he poked my leg. "You got any pain?"

"Only when I try to pull it out," I said.

"I'll pack ice around your ankle to keep down the swelling," he said.

"Sport," my dad yelled. "You're in good hands. I'll be right back after the Congressman's speech."

"See you later, Daddy-O," I said. I didn't want him to feel guilt over leaving.

"He's a big-picture man," I told Gus.

"He paints them?" Gus said.

"No," I said. "He keeps his mind on them. That means figuring out all the things his boss needs to do every day so, in the end, he can win the election."

"What kind of things?" Gus asked.

"Making speeches and getting on TV in Florida so people remember to vote for him," I said.

"Guess what, King Tut?" Sam shouted. "Reporters are here!"

"Looks like that Congressman should stick with you if he wants to be on TV," Gus said.

"I already know the lady from the *Hill Rag* newspaper," I said. "She came to another situation I had."

The TV people kept asking Gus to do something

more interesting than putting ice on my leg. "Come on," a camera guy said, "we need footage."

"If he could show you footage, he would," Lucy Rose said. "His footage is the problem."

It turns out footage is a TV word that means action pictures. They got plenty when a firelady wrapped a chain around one side of the V of the tree and hooked the ends to the truck bumper. Then she drove backward for a few inches.

"Does it feel looser?" Gus asked me.

"Tighter, actually," I said.

"Back up!" Gus yelled.

The firemen were stumped. They called the city. The city called their tree man, who called the fire chief, who told everybody the expert's opinion. "He says our best bet is to cut it off."

"Absolutely not!" my mom said.

This time I was glad she stuck up for me.

"We're talking about the branch, ma'am," the chief said. "We all agree the foot should remain with the leg."

While the rescuers talked to each other, the

reporters talked to me. The Channel 7 lady was the best. She asked about my bravery. The man from Channel 4 asked my mom what she thought. She said, "For the life of me I cannot understand what would make him want to climb in a tree in the first place."

Later, when it was dark, Gus let me use his flashlight. I spotlighted Mr. Neenobber and his spoon. Then I shined it on Ashley. She was picking her nose and pretending she was itching it. "Girls never admit to nose-picking," I told Gus.

"Or farting," he said.

If my foot hadn't been stuck I would have fallen out of the tree from laughing.

When Sam's dad and his baby sister, Julia, came Mr. Alswang said "Hello up there" to me and "Get your stuff" to Sam and "I told your mom I'd give you a ride home" to Jonique. Julia only said one thing but she said it over and over. "Uppie, uppie, uppie."

"She wants to get in the tree with me," I called down.

"No chance for that," Mr. Alswang said.

Sam and Jonique wanted to stay on the sidewalk but begging doesn't work on Sam's dad.

That conversation reminded Pop to send Lucy Rose inside to put on her pajamas.

"I'll wave at you when I'm brushing my teeth," she said.

Gus looked at me and said, "Your teeth are chattering." He swooped down in the picker box and came back up with a silver space blanket.

"Hey," I said. "This is made of Mylar like those balloons that stay puffed for weeks."

"How did you know that?" Gus said.

"I have a collection of airless balloons," I said. "But I never knew they could keep me warm."

"Wrap it around yourself," he said. "Bodies get cold faster when they aren't moving."

"My foot is cold and it hurts," I said.

"How much?" Gus asked.

"Not as much as when I crashed my knee into Mr. Levy's brick wall," I said. "More than the time I jumped off a ledge at the National Cathedral and Dr. Stroud had to glue my chin back together."

"I'm glad you're in pain," he said.

I looked at him.

"It means your blood is reaching your toes," he said.

"I think cold water is too," I said.

"More likely you have a shoe full of sweat," he said.

"Cool!" I said.

"Gus," the chief said, "use your jigsaw to cut away the bark closest to his ankle."

"Yipes," I said. "Be careful."

You'd think Gus sawing would be great footage but the reporters left me for a fire hydrant explosion in Tenleytown. All the firefighters, except for Gus and Frank, went to soak up the flood. Who knows where the police went? I don't. At 9:17, the only people left were Pop, two ambulance guys named Lamar and Thomas, Mr. Neenobber, Mr.

Lee, and Mr. Lee's Great Dane. Even my own mother had gone inside with Madam.

"Am I being abandoned?" I said.

"Never," Gus said. "Frank had a brainstorm. Takoma Park firefighters are coming to give us a hand."

"And my foot, I hope," I said.

The only one who answered me was the Great Dane. I barked back.

"Sounds like you're a born barker," Gus told me.

"It's easy," I said. "Bark while you're inhaling. If you do it while you're breathing out it sounds fake."

We practiced barking until my mom came racing outside. She thought wild dogs could be on the loose. Luckily, that was when my dad came back.

Unluckily, that was also when it thundered so loud our brains shook. And it rained so hard Gus's mustache turned into a little waterfall. "The wind snatched my space blanket," I said.

"Betty," my dad yelled, "go inside. I'll bring umbrellas back out."

He also brought a raincoat for me.

"This is Lucy Rose's," I said.

"She doesn't mind," my dad said.

"I do. It's decorated," I said, "with pink dots and red fringe."

"Let me tell you the rule of men," Gus said. "Whatever will save us is what we wear."

"Like what?" I asked.

"Like helmets, boots, fireproof pants, and smoke masks," he said.

"Anybody would want to wear that stuff," I said.

"Not always," Gus said. "They're heavy. They smell. They're hot. But I'll tell you what, if protecting myself meant I had to wear my underwear on my head, I'd have on a Fruit of the Loom hat right now."

"As long as you don't have to wear a sports jacket," I said. That was a joke.

I put on the dotty coat but I told them, "Do not tell Lucy Rose or anybody that I wore this girl coat and if the reporters come back I'm taking it off."

The storm stopped after a while but the tree kept leaking water on us. Gus held Pop's big umbrella over our heads. "I'm holding mine sideways to block wind," I said.

After eleven minutes my arm felt like my bones were bending. The other parts of me felt fed up with the whole disaster.

Then Gus's friends drove up. "Oh, no!" I said. "ANOTHER cherry picker!"

"Yo! Henry, Nate!" Gus yelled. "Did you bring it?"

"Sure did," Nate said. "We'll be up in a flash."

"Hey! Guess what?" I said. "When you yell into

an umbrella, it sounds louder than when you yell into plain air."

"Seriously?" Gus asked.

"Totally," I said. "Listen."

"I wonder why it does that," Gus said.

"Beats me," I said.

Finally, at 11:11 p.m., Nate and Henry and Gus freed my foot. When it popped out it made a sound like *thwook* and it felt exactly like a miracle. Also numb. "Riding in a cherry picker is as exciting as I always thought it would be," I told Gus.

I also got to ride on a rolling bed. Thomas steered it into the ambulance. They had a tank of oxygen, a blood pressure measurer, and special cloth that stops bleeding. Lamar used crooked scissors to cut my shoelaces all the way up. Then he cut off the tongue and gave it to me. Thomas peeled my high-top off. Then they warmed my foot with an electric towel and poked my toes to see if they had feeling. They did. Lamar squirted Neosporin on me and wound a stretchy lime green bandage around my foot and up my leg. My dad patted my arm. I think that was because he was glad.

"Where are my crutches?" I asked.

"You don't need them," Thomas said. "What you need is to walk." That was disappointing news.

The first walking I did was to Gus. "Thanks for the rescue," I said.

"Glad to do it," Gus said. "It was the first time we ever used the Jaws of Life to get a boy out of a tree."

3

STARRING ME

This morning, my mom drove me to school. Lucy Rose, Jonique, and Sam were waiting by the main door. Lucy Rose clapped when I got out of the car. Jonique carried my books. Sam had the most questions.

"How was it being saved by the Jaws of Life?"

"The greatest," I said. "For me and for the firemen. Before my foot situation they only used the Jaws to open car doors that were smashed in accidents."

"What do the Jaws look like?" Sam asked.

"They're kind of like a jackhammer," I said.

"There's a cutter part that they didn't use and a spreader part that they did. I never thought wood could stretch but the Jaws made the hole open enough to squeeze my foot out."

"How did it look?" Jonique asked.

"Soggy," I told her.

"How come?" she asked.

"Because every foot has about a hundred and twenty-five *thousand* sweat glands," I said. "All of mine were working."

"Stink-o-rama," Lucy Rose said.

"Totally," I said. "My mom said my shoe is ruined. I told her, 'Not to me.' I nailed it to the wall over my bed so I will always have the memory."

"Does your whole room smell like foot?" Sam asked.

"Completely," I said. "Come over and have a smell."

Lucy Rose twisted her face so her nose and freckles were bunched up. "Never in this lifetime," she said.

"This afternoon for me," Sam said.

At school, Mrs. Timony got a chair from the teachers' lounge to prop up my leg. Then she said, "Adam, do you feel up to telling us what happened?"

I didn't leave anything out, except for the part when I was feeling sad.

"Notice Adam's attention to detail," Mrs. Timony told our class. "The small things are what makes a story come alive."

"Here's a big detail," I said. "When everybody was gone except for Gus, my dad, Pop, the firemen,

and the ambulance guys, I got to pee out of the tree."

That announcement made the girls act deranged. The boys thought it was the best part of the whole adventure.

"It is possible to have too many details, Adam," Mrs. Timony said.

4

THE CHALLENGE OF MY LIFE

*T*his morning my mom took off my green bandage. Even worse, my foot was back to normal. Mrs. Timony said she was glad and took the rolling chair back to the lounge. From the way everybody was acting you'd think they forgot about my foot. The day didn't get better until after we finished writing our nonfiction book reviews. Our science teacher came to visit our class. You can tell when Mr. Santalices is feeling enthusiastic because he flaps his arms. When he told us about Challenge America!, he looked like one of the Wright brothers about to fly off the cliff. But at the end he

settled down and got serious. "The Challenge isn't for everyone," he said.

That made me think it was for me.

"When you wake up in the morning, what is the first thing you think about?" Mr. Santalices asked.

"Things I want to invent," I said. "Or explode."

"*Bueno!*" he said. "Anyone else feel that way?"

"Sam does," Lucy Rose said.

"Samuel?" Mr. S said. "Do you like to make things?"

"I've made some really bad smells before," Sam said.

"We all do from time to time," Mr. Santalices said.

"I mean with chemicals," Sam said. "I made a concoction that was so stinkola we had to open all the windows and go out for dinner. When we came home it still smelled so terrible my mom got a headache."

"Curiosity is a gift," Mr. Santalices said.

Kathleen raised her hand and said, "I'm curious."

"Magnificent," Mr. Santalices said.

Then he said, "Adam, please return your chair to the normal sitting position."

"Don't worry," I said. "I'm good at balancing on the back legs."

"Down," Mr. Santalices said.

"Sorry," I said. "I can't help it. It happens automatically."

Mr. S kept going. "This year's Challenge is called 'REINVENTIONS: Recycling the Old into the New.' That means combining things that already exist to create something new, original, and useful."

"I don't get it," Josh said.

"Well," Mr. S said, "in the old days, kids would use two cans, invented to hold food, and string, invented to tie things together, to make something new—a toy telephone."

"Cool," Pierra said.

"It didn't work very well," Mr. Santalices said. "I expect your reinventions will be better."

"Hey," Hannah said. "I could sew the motor from my brother's remote-control race car into a mitten and make a remote-control duster!"

"Terrific idea!" Mr. Santalices said.

Who knew that regular old Hannah Banana was a genius? I didn't.

"You can work alone or in teams of two students. You may tell your parents your ideas and they may take you to buy supplies. Parents CANNOT come up with the idea or design it or help build it."

"But projects come out a lot better when they help," Josh said.

"Part of the Challenge is for students to help each other," Mr. S said. He pointed at Ashley. "Are you ready?"

"I'm sure I could invent," she said. "If I felt like it. Which I don't because it's a waste of time."

"I'm glad Thomas Edison's time wasn't so valuable or we'd be having this chat in the dark," Mr. S said.

Ashley swung her braids. "He didn't have anything else to do. TV probably didn't exist back then."

"You're right," Mr. Santalices said. "I think having no TV must have really bothered Mr. Edison, because after he invented the first long-lasting lightbulb, he came up with a movie projector."

"It's good we have lights and movies but most things that get invented are things I don't ever use," Ashley said.

"Joseph Gayetty would disagree," Mr. S said.

"Who is Joseph Gayetty?" Ashley said.

"The inventor of toilet paper!" I shouted. "But Zeth Wheeler was the one that thought up the idea of making it in a roll with squares that tear off."

"Way to go, Joe!" Sam said.

"Is toilet paper a reinvention?" I asked. "Because paper was invented before."

"I suppose in a way it is," Mr. Santalices said. "How do you know so much?"

"I study inventors," I said. "Also toilets."

"A fascinating and unexpected combination," Mr. Santalices said.

"Thanks," I said. "One day I am going to visit the Museum of Toilets."

"There's no such thing," Bart Bigelow said.

"It's in India," I told him.

That made the whole class laugh. Bart said something I couldn't hear. I wish I did because Lucy Rose told him, "That is not appropriate in the extreme."

I like not appropriate.

"I'm still not reinventing," Ashley said.

"I understand," Mr. Santalices said. "Not everyone wants the chance to ride on the Winners' Bus to the Washington Metropolitan

Area Region 6 semifinals convention in Chantilly, Virginia, and present their reinvention to the judges, and stay overnight at the Marriott Hotel."

"Is there a pool at that hotel?" Amir asked.

"Do they have continental breakfasts?" Marisol called out.

"Yes to both questions," Mr. Santalices said.

"What else does the winner get?" Ashley asked.

"The first-place winner from our school will get a certificate suitable for framing, a blue ribbon, and the trip to Chantilly," Mr. S said. "The first-place regional winner will receive a handsome trophy, a hundred-dollar savings bond, and a trip to Philadelphia for the national competition. The person or team who wins that Challenge gets the grand prize, a trip to New York City, and they will demonstrate their reinvention on the *Every Day in the USA* television show."

"Why didn't you say so?" Ashley asked. "You can sign me up now. I have decided to win."

"Hey," I said. "I'm the one that has TV experience."

"Give it up, Melonhead," she said. Then she looked at me like I was some pipsqueak.

"Give it your best," Mr. Santalices told our class. "Think big thoughts. Ask yourselves: What old inventions can I combine to make life better? Easier? Safer? More fun?"

"I'm already wondering," I said.

"That's the winning spirit," Mr. S said. "Everyone who is interested in taking the Challenge gets a logbook."

That turned out to be everybody.

"Report as you go," he told us. "Start with the time and date. Describe what you are doing, measure your ingredients, and list your supplies. Write down a step-by-step record of everything you do."

On the board he wrote:

Bow-tie-tying machine
Supplies: Bow tie, 1 D battery, wire, paper clips, clothespins, small motor

"Who would own a bow tie?" Ashley said.

"I would and I do," Mr. S said. "The next step is

to illustrate your idea." He drew a hilarious picture of the tie-tying machine.

"If your reinvention works, test and retest to see if it's foolproof," he said.

"What if it's a bust?" Bart asked.

"Write down why you think it failed and your ideas about how to fix it," Mr. Santalices said, "and try again."

He made a cartoon of a man whose head was about to explode. Underneath the guy's strangled neck it said: "Problem: Ties tie too tight."

That made me crack up, which made my chair legs slide. I had to save myself by grabbing my desk. But I over-yanked so I crashed backwards into Alexandra Mendelsohn's chair. "Sorry!" I said. "It was a total accident. I didn't know I was doing it."

"Four on the floor, Adam," Mr. S said. To the class he said, "We'll meet next week."

On the walk home Sam and I ate his pretzels and the Count Chocula from my pocket. We talked about Hannah's amazing idea. "We should be a team," Sam said.

"Two brains are better than Hannah's," I said.

"I hope," Sam said.

"We've been inventing since we were kids. Hannah's a lucky beginner," I said.

For the rest of the day all I could think about was what to invent and what to eat. For dinner I ate eleven fish sticks, nine baby carrots, zero peas, and vanilla cream pie that was still frozen because I couldn't wait. I'm probably having a growth spurt right this minute.

Before I could invent I had to do language arts homework. We had to write four paragraphs about a personal experience. I combed my brain and finally I remembered an experience that my mom said was extremely personal. I did the title in red so it would stand out, plus two illustrations.

At bedtime I made a tent out of my sheets and crawled under it with a bowl of crunchy peanut butter mixed with grape jam and a tube of Ritz crackers. To make it more like camping I always use my finger as a spreader and my mattress for a plate. After I ate four, I put the rest under my pillow for a midnight snack.

A good fact: Average kids eat fifteen hundred

peanut butter and jelly sandwiches before they are grown up. I am not average. I had eaten that many by the time I was in second grade. That doesn't even count my triple-decker cracker sandwiches.

Next, I shined all my flashlights on myself so I could read in the dark about Walter Hunt, inventor of the safety pin. Guess why he did it? For

money, that's why. He owed somebody fifteen dollars so he had to come up with something.

My plan was to stay awake until my dad got home so I could tell him my Challenge news. But every time I checked, the dome light was still on. Probably because Buddy Boyd is trying to get the other Congresspeople to vote for his bill. Then Florida can get millions of bucks to clean up the Everglades. I hope he wins because that is the best swamp I've ever been in. Plus, if it disappears, think of all the alligators and snakes that will be homeless.

I fell asleep too soon. And when I woke up this morning I felt like my face was lying in gravel. But it was only busted peanut butter crackers that were stuck to my cheek and hair.

5
THE UMASVFSW

The only excellent thing about parent-teacher conferences is that we get off from school. That gave Sam and me all of yesterday to search for supplies. We hit such a major jackpot in his basement that by the time Mrs. Alswang called us upstairs for matzo ball soup, we only needed one thing.

We found it at my house, in my mom's pink zip-up purse that's for her makeup. I put it in my sweatshirt pocket. Sam stuffed his pockets with apples so we wouldn't die from hunger while we were gluing and sawing in his basement.

Our project came out so well that I could

not stop thinking about it last night. Today, the excitement of yesterday made it feel like school lasted for fifteen days. The only laughing we did was when the boys rushed through the state capitals song. The girls tried to keep up and by the time we got to Dover, Delaware, the whole thing fell apart. The other fun part was pasteling my self-portrait. I gave myself a mustache.

The rest of the day was no good. We had to review multiplication tables because a quiz is coming. Then Mr. Pitt gave a talk about Respecting School Property.

"This means that NO ONE should be going into the boys' bathroom and THROWING wads of wet TOILET PAPER at the ceiling," he said. "No doubt it seems funny when it FALLS on the head of an unsuspecting student, but it most certainly is NOT."

He was wrong about that. Just saying it made our whole class laugh like monkeys. Especially me.

"Mr. Johnson does not enjoy scraping dried-up tissue off the ceiling," Mr. Pitt said.

Then he gave me an unpleasant stare. He is

always suspecting me of things I didn't do. Also, some things that I did do. At the conference he told my parents about one of them and my mom was disappointed to hear it.

Sam whispered at the back of my head, "He probably thinks you clumped up the ceiling because you're a toilet paper expert."

On the way home we stopped to show Pop how our reinventing was going so far. He was sitting on the side porch, reading a book about Grover Cleveland, who was an ancient president. Jonique was crawling around the yard, looking for four-leaf clovers. Lucy Rose was watering the pansies. She sprayed us, of course.

"Lucy Rose!" Pop said.

"I'm making them feel like they're refreshed," she said.

"It worked," I said. "Thanks."

Sam and I jumped over the fence and climbed halfway over the porch railing so we could sit with one leg on each side like we were riding horses. "You can still see Jaw scrapings on the magnolia," I said.

"I imagine that will be true for years to come," Pop said.

That made me feel important.

"Would you like a bowl of Madam's homemade yogurt?"

"No," Sam and I said at the same time.

I unzipped my backpack and pulled out a short plastic pipe that was left over from the Alswangs' new bathroom. Sam got two curved plastic pipes out of his. "These are called elbows," he said.

Pop bent his arms and pointed them at us. "So are these," he said.

We put the plastic elbows on the ends of the straight pipe so the whole thing looked like a stretched-out Z. I held one elbow up to Pop's eye.

"I'll be bamboozled," he said. "I see the Hacketts' chimney."

"It's actually a reflection of the Hacketts' chimney," Sam said. "Inside the pipes are two round mirrors that came out of Mrs. Melon's face powder kit."

"This is a mighty fine periscope," Pop said. "But how is it a reinvention?"

"Sorry to say, it's not," Lucy Rose said. She was hanging upside down off the porch railing, faking like she was going to fall.

"We know," I said. "Thomas Doughty built his periscope over a hundred years ago. This is only one part of our masterpiece. Look at our design."

"Look but don't comment," Lucy Rose told Pop. "Adults are not allowed to give one speck of help."

Sam showed him the drawing in our log. "All we need are nails, glass, bike pedals, Mylar balloons, cup holders, wood, paint, and helium gas," he said. "We already have glue."

Pop's face looked impressed.

"You are overwhelmed by our amazing brains," I said.

"That I am," Pop said. "I don't know anyone else who would think of building a wooden submarine."

"It's called the Underwater Magnifying and Spying Vehicle for Shallow Water. To make it easy we call it the UMASVFSW," Sam said. "We got the idea last year when we took our first tour of the FBI."

"Now that we've been on sixteen tours we know plenty about catching crooks," I said. "The FBI knows us, too. We send them letters with spy-catching advice."

"I don't get it," Jonique said. "What do crooks have to do with your invention?"

I had to explain. "Say some spies are discussing their evil plans near the Reflecting Pool. If they spot the Capitol Police, the spies can just change the topic to lima beans and act like they work at the Department of Agriculture. But this way they will be truthful because they'll never know they are being watched from the middle of the Reflecting Pool by a lip-reading FBI agent."

"A regular sub would be way too big for the Reflecting Pool," Sam said.

"I'll say this," Pop said. "The UMASVFSW beats the submarine Cornelius van Drebbel built in the 1620s."

"Does it ever," I said. "His submarine was really a boat covered with leather."

"Which is not the most waterproof," Lucy Rose said.

"Wood is," Sam said.

"Also rowing underwater is a terrible idea because it's bound to leak," I said.

"Putting in the air tubes showed sharp thinking but they had to row in the dark," Sam said.

"Ours is going to have a skylight and after we win, we're donating the UMASVFSW to the government," I said.

"You are great patriots," Pop said.

"Thank you," I said.

6
LUCKILY AND UNLUCKILY

The after-school plan was for me, Sam, Jonique, and Lucy Rose to put all our money together and go to Baking Divas for a snack. But when the bell rang, Mrs. Timony let everybody go except me. She said I should go to the principal's office. That felt like a disaster.

Walking down the hall, I could feel my sweat. "You guys wait for me outside," I told Sam.

"Good luck, Chuck," he said.

After, when I told them what happened, Sam said, "How did she know about it already?"

"I guess Mrs. Timony told her," I said.

"She'll probably tell Mr. Pitt," Jonique said.

"She said she was going to," I told her.

"Let's get to the cupcakes," Lucy Rose said.

Madam was standing in front of the Divas' store and under her arm was a dog that was smaller than a meat loaf. "This is Rex," she said. "And he's driving me crazy."

"Is he yours?" Jonique asked.

"Oh, no. I'm dog-sitting while the Rosens are in China. But until they get back I have to carry him everywhere because he is an escape artist. We can't let him play in the yard because he slips between the fence bars and runs down the street. Pop had to nab him twice today."

Dogs are not allowed in bakeries, so Madam gave us money to buy the Berry Cherry Tart she needed for her dinner party and coffee that she needed for herself. For a reward we got to pick one snack each and she paid. I got a Vanilla Swirling Dervish cupcake with caramel inside. "These are actually better than Hostess Sno-Balls," I told the Divas.

We ate at one of the outside tables. Madam said anyone who wanted could walk with her to Frager's Hardware store to buy two brass hinges for Pop.

"I love hardware," I said. "But I can't go."

When I told her why she said, "You'd better get home and tell your mom."

I did and the minute I opened the door I yelled, "I have fresh news from the principal!"

"Oh, dear," my mom said.

I waited for three seconds. Then I said, "I won Homework of the Week!"

"It's a dream come true," my mom said, and hugged me until I had to plead for relief so I could breathe. "Homework of the week?! You did the best job in the whole school?"

"Lucy Rose said it was the shock of this lifetime," I said.

"Nonsense," my mom said. "I always knew you would do great things in your life."

"I have to go do another great thing," I said. "It's for the Challenge America! Sam and I are meeting at Madam and Pop's."

Sam was already there, trying to borrow Pop's

measuring tape. "We need to see how deep the Reflecting Pool is," he told Pop. "I'm not allowed to use my dad's because last time I left it completely stretched out in the yard."

I explained the problem. "It got rusty and it won't zing back when you push the button. But we have to find out how tall to make the UMASVFSW."

"You may take my folding measuring stick," Pop said. "It's made of wood."

"May we borrow Gumbo, too?" Sam asked.

"Certainly," Pop said. "He's got an eye for spies."

It took fifty-two minutes to run eleven blocks because Gumbo flopped down in front of the Old Senate Office Building. We had to bribe him with Honeycomb cereal from my pocket.

When we finally got there, Sam measured and I wrote. Getting home went quicker. Gumbo was pulling his leash

and his leash was pulling me so fast the toes of my newest sneakers got scraped.

"For a poodle, Gumbo has no patience," Sam said.

He ran even faster on the last block because he had to capture Rex, who had squeezed through the fence. Lucy Rose was trying to stop him but he was running in circles around her red boots. Whichever side she turned to was the wrong one. But when Gumbo got behind Lucy Rose and barked, Rex jumped back through the fence in a second and ran straight for Madam's lap.

"How did it go?" Pop asked us.

"The water is only eighteen inches deep," I said.

"You'll need a very short FBI agent to operate that submarine," he said.

"A tour guide told us it is thirty inches in the middle," Sam said. "But that's still not deep enough. I'm forty-nine inches standing up."

"Plus we figured out it's not exactly a reinvention because it's supposed to do what a submarine already does," I said.

"If we turned a submarine into a giant ice cream maker, that would be a reinvention," Sam said.

"Or if you turned it into a sandwich," Lucy Rose said.

"You're hilarious," Sam said, like she wasn't.

"Keep thinking," Pop said. "Most experiments pay off eventually."

"It already did," I said. "Now I know it takes six million, seven hundred fifty thousand gallons to fill the Reflecting Pool. That's a fact anybody would like."

"You should cheer yourself right up," Lucy Rose told us. "On account of fitting a submarine on the bus to Chantilly would wear you down to your bones."

When I got home my dad was in a Zip-a-Dee-Doo-Dah mood and it got even better when I told him about my Homework of the Week. My mom cooked cheeseburgers with double pickles and BBQ sauce for dinner because I won. I knew it was a big celebration because she usually likes to cook things that don't stain.

"We're mighty proud of you, Sport," my dad said.

"Tell us about your winning homework, darling," my mom said.

"Nope," I said. "You can read it for yourself. Tomorrow it's going on display on the bulletin board by the principal's office."

"How exciting," my mom said. "Everyone will see it there."

"We'll call Grammy and Gramps after dessert," my dad said.

7
AUTHOR! AUTHOR!

"*I* wish I could go with you two," my dad said.

"That's okay," I told him. "You have to keep your eyes on the big picture."

"Exactly right," he said.

Then he told my mom, "Take pictures, Betty. Big and little. Close up and far away. Front and side."

"Of course," she said. "This is a red-letter day."

I'm not clear about what that means but it's good. Here's how I know: Usually my mom wears mom clothes. Today she had on a blue shirt with a sweater that matches and black pants and high heels and a flowered scarf going around her neck.

"Mom, don't go insane," I said. "Jonique has gotten Homework of the Week about ten times."

"Homework of the Week is a huge honor, Adam," she said. "Let's get going so I can see it."

At school Mrs. McBee was coming down the stairs when we were starting up. "Congratulations, Adam!" she said. "I just read your homework. I love it!"

My mom smiled and said, "You're sweet to say so, Lola."

After that it was like I was in a praise avalanche. My third-grade teacher, Mr. Welsh, said, "You captured the experience, Adam. Good job!" Sam's dad gave me a high five. Mr. Johnson said, "I never read anything like that before." Mrs. Boxley said, "I cannot wait to have you in my class next year!"

Lucy Rose came out screaming, "Melonhead! Your homework is the star of the bulletin board. It has the comment of: 'Excellent details! Good use of adjectives!'"

My mom squeezed me into a shoulder hug and said, "We'd better go see what all these compliments are about."

Inside it sounded like a party. Parents were giving me thumbs-ups. Mr. Gold yelled, "Author! Author!" Ashley's mom swished my hair with her hand and told my mom, "Your son is a gem."

"Thank you, Rhonda," my mom said.

"Follow me to my masterpiece, Mom," I said.

When we got to the board my mom's face got red and her eyelids bugged out with pride. She read my title out loud. " 'My Personal Experience with Head Lice.' "

"Look at my completely lifelike but magnified picture of a louse," I said. "The dots are nits."

My mom whispered, "You didn't."

"I did so," I said. "How can you forget my head lice? Dad had to shampoo me in the yard. Aunt Cindy had to drive from Baltimore to inspect our heads. You boiled the whole house."

My mom made a loud inhale. "Your head lice are not something we talk about in public."

"You're the one that said they were personal," I said.

My mom looked at her high heels.

"Personal," she said, "meaning private."

"I thought personal meant it happened to you personally," I said.

"Kids get head lice," Josh's mom said. "There's no reason to be ashamed."

"Why would I feel ashamed?" I asked. "I think they're interesting."

My mom was having a breathing attack.

Mrs. Rangoon patted her. "Adam might have caught them from Amir," she said.

"We put our heads together a lot," Amir said.

"Or from Elton," a third-grade dad said.

"Or from the triplets," the triplets' mom said.

"But Adam was the only kid smart enough to write about it," Lucy Rose said.

What I felt was confused. "Are you proud, Mom?" I asked.

My mom put her arm around my shoulders. "I am," she said. "But the next time you write a story, I want to read it ahead of time."

8

THE GREATEST THING
WE EVER FOUND

For lunch my dad fixed Sam and me bacon and peanut butter sandwiches. It is his only recipe. We are only allowed to eat them on Sundays because my mom thinks they clog up your heart. She eats Light n' Lively instead.

"We need a great invention that will get us to Chantilly," Sam told my parents.

"It's already been invented," my dad said. "It's called a car."

"Who needs a car?" I said. "When we win the Challenge we'll get to go by bus."

"Tell me your best idea," he said.

"We don't have a new one yet," Sam said.

"How about inventing something that will sweep the nation and make us rich?" my dad said.

"Something that will sweep the nation is an outstanding idea!" Sam said.

"What do you think, Betty?" my dad asked.

"I'm in favor of any invention that doesn't stain, involve a tree, cause bleeding, or have anything to do with head lice," she said.

My brain started planning on the spot. "You're going to love it, Mom," I said. "Our Sweep the Nation invention will clean everything it touches. It will be like having someone do your hobby for you."

Then Sam reminded me, "We're not allowed to use ideas that come from parents. Even great ones."

"Great parents or great ideas?" my dad said.

"Both," I said.

"Let's go, Moe," Sam said to me. "We think better when we're moving."

We talked while we stomped in puddles left over from last night's rain. When we passed Lucy

Rose's house her mom invited us to help dig holes for planting her yellow flowers.

"We can't," I said. "We're inventing today."

"Same with me," Lucy Rose said. "I'm building a roll-up fence made of paint stirrers that will trap Rex in the yard. I might get to use the drill if I get under Pop's supervision."

"You are one hundred percent lucky," Sam said.

Drizzle started around A Street but we didn't get lured away from the Challenge until Seward Square. That was because when the weather is perfect like today, that park is the all-time best place for mud surfing. I took a flying leap.

"Jump back, Jack!" I screamed.

Luckily, Sam did. I landed on the muddy path near the bus stop and skied for at least ten feet on my new high-tops. He skied after me, yelling, "I win the gold medal for speed and distance."

Then his foot hit a tree root and he shot up in the air and landed facedown in the wet grass.

"Have a nice TRIP?" I asked.

"See you next FALL!" Sam said. He was laughing and spitting mud at the same time. All of a sudden he started speed-crawling. "Bony macaroni," he whispered. "You won't believe it!"

Right there, winding through the muddy grass, was a garter snake. It was as skinny as a fat pencil, longer than a ruler, and slithering fast. I flopped down flat in the sopping grass. "I'll make a wall around him with my arms and face," I told Sam. "You capture him."

"Here, snakie, snakie," Sam said.

"Hurry up," I said, "it's heading for my lips."

Sam's hand pounced. He grabbed the snake by its waist.

"This is the first snake on the loose I've seen in

Washington, D.C.," I said. "In Florida they're easy to find."

"What a great state!" Sam said.

"Stuff it in your coat pocket," I said. "Gently. And keep your hand over the opening."

"From all the wiggling going on in there, I think he's trying to escape," Sam said.

In case wiggling was a sign of hunger I got two Frankenberries out of my pocket and dropped them into Sam's.

"Let's go across the street to the Conroys'," I said. "There is something about owning a snake that makes me want to show off."

Sam rang their doorbell without stopping until Mickey answered. He is mostly Sam's friend but also mine. I know him from when we took Experiments with Food in aftercare.

"Stand clear for snake delivery!" I yelled.

"This is our lucky day," Mrs. Conroy said.

Mickey and his little brother, Jimmy, were wearing Sunday pants and nothing else. "We're going to Temple Sinai because it's our babysitter's wedding," Jimmy said. "But first I need to see a snake."

Before Sam could fish it out, Mrs. Conroy pointed at a pile of clothes and said, "Gentlemen, no socks, no shoes, no snake." She is a teacher so she has a way of making kids do things.

Mickey dressed in a flash but Jimmy's shirt had buttons. Then his sock twisted. "No looking until I'm done," Jimmy said. "Right, Mom?"

"Right," Mrs. Conroy said.

"What's your snake's name?" Mickey asked.

"Cobra," I said.

"That is perfect," he said.

Mr. Conroy came down the stairs carrying a box from Richey's shoes.

"This could make a fine snake condo," he said.

"I'll say it will," I told him. "Especially since we're bringing him to school tomorrow."

"It's a surprise for Mrs. Timony," Sam said.

"She certainly will be surprised," Mrs. Conroy said while she mashed Jimmy's loafer onto his foot.

"She will go Cobra crazy," Mickey said.

"I'm done," Jimmy said. "Show me."

I plopped Cobra in the shoe box so everybody could see at once. He got a lot of praise but Jimmy was the Conroy with the truest comment. "It's the best thing you could own except a penguin," he said.

"He's a snake charmer," I said.

"I'll get Cobra a circle of bologna," Jimmy said. "We're all out of snake food."

"We never even had any snake food," Mickey said.

"Here, Jimmy," I said. "You can be the one who pokes breathing holes in the box."

When we were leaving, Mr. Conroy said, "Adam, I heard you won Homework of the Week. Congratulations!"

"Thanks!" I said. "Writing is easier than I thought."

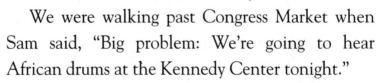

"A good topic makes the difference," Mr. Conroy said.

We were walking past Congress Market when Sam said, "Big problem: We're going to hear African drums at the Kennedy Center tonight."

"That's no problem," I said. "I love African drums."

"Everybody loves them," Sam said. "I just don't

think Cobra should be all alone on his first night in my house."

"My mom would flip over if she saw a snake," I said. "That would really upset Cobra."

Thank the lucky stars for Pop. "Cobra can live with me while Madam is visiting her sister in New Jersey," he said. "But she's coming home soon so first thing in the morning it's vamoose, snake."

"What do they say when a moose has to leave?" I asked him.

"Vamoose, moose?"

"We'll pick him up on the way to school," Sam said.

"Problem Two," I said. "The thrills of finding a pet blocked the Challenge from our minds."

"We'll catch up," Sam said.

When I got home my dad was at a Floridians for Fishing meeting. My mom was disappointed because she thinks Sunday should be family time. I was disappointed because I couldn't tell my dad about Cobra.

9

COBRA THE MAGNIFICENT

My dad went to work a little late so he could eat Betty's Famous Scrambled Eggs and Cheese Casserole with us. To do my share of cooking, I peeled three clementines. Then I ate my before-breakfast Cocoa Puffs and drank the leftover chocolate milk out of the bowl. "How's the reinventing going?" my dad asked.

"Not so well," I said. I wanted to tell him about Cobra but to be thoughtful to my mom, I didn't.

She was not so thoughtful to me. When I was filling my pocket with Honey Nut Cheerios my mom snuck up and sprayed natural bug spray on all my uncovered skin.

"Now I smell like Grammy," I said.

"Grammy smells good," she said.

"For a lady," I said.

"Sorry," she said. "Mosquito season is coming and you have tender skin. I don't want them to eat you alive."

"You just gave me an idea!" I said, and ran before she could spray again.

We had a slow walk to Pop's because Sam's backpack was full of rock samples. Mostly quartz. Mine was light. All it had was a library book and the ingredients for our new invention. When I explained my idea to Sam he said, "It's even better than our wooden submarine."

"Anytime, Frankenstein," I said. "My brain is an Idea-O-Matic."

At Pop's, Cobra was ready and waiting on the radiator cover.

"I put crumpled newspaper in his condo so he'd have a place to hide," Pop said.

"Thanks," I said.

But when we got down the block I asked Sam, "Does Cobra look skinnier to you?"

"Snakes are skinny," he said.

Guess who we saw on Independence Avenue, swinging her braids and waiting for the light to change? Ashley the Annoyer, that's who.

"What's in that box?" she asked.

"You'll see after morning greetings," Sam said.

"It's your invention!" Ashley screamed.

"It is not but you still can't look until we say so," I told her.

"That's not fair," Ashley said, and dropped her sparkly purple lunch bag on the sidewalk.

She thinks a lot of things aren't fair even when they are.

"Open it!" she said, like a demand.

"Nope," Sam said. "You have to wait."

"I do not," Ashley said.

She ran around me and jumped in front of Sam. "Too slow," she said, and swooped to grab the top off.

"NOT too slow," he said, and passed the box to me.

I didn't do anything to her but Ashley toppled

over backwards and landed on her flowery back-pack. She looked like a flipped-over turtle.

"Definitely too slow," Sam said.

"When we get to school, I'm telling on you," she screamed. "You'll have to go to Mr. Pitt's office and suffer."

"You don't have anything to tell," I said.

"You could have BROKEN my back in two and made me get a concussion of the head!" She yelled so loud that two ladies stared at us.

At school, Mrs. Timony told Ashley to stop dwelling on her head and to take a seat. Then she sent Clayton Briggs to the library to ask Mrs. Ochmanek if we could borrow all the books about garter snakes. All turned out to be one.

Kathleen got to read about care but when she got to the feeding, Pierra said, "Revolting."

Jonique said, "Totally P-U."

Then all the girls had a meltdown.

"I cannot believe snakes eat mice," Lucy Rose said. "That's inhuman."

"It's reptilian," Mrs. Timony said.

Then without even looking at me she said, "Adam, if you keep leaning backwards in your chair the only safe place I can put you will be the floor."

"Cool!" I said. Then I figured out that she meant it to be a warning.

"The book says snakes need warm spaces,"

Kathleen told the class. "They can live under a lightbulb."

Josh waved his arms. "Pick me! I'll set it up!"

"Pierra," Mrs. Timony said. "Please put my desk lamp on the table next to the book basket."

"Okay," Pierra said. "But I'm not moving the snake."

"Hannah may have that honor," Mrs. Timony said.

"When we lived in London my cousin Charley had a pet snake," Hannah told us.

"Wonderful! A student with experience," Mrs. Timony said. "What did you learn?"

"That I don't fancy snakes," Hannah said.

"Cobra is as plain as a snake can be," Sam said.

"In England 'fancy' means the same as 'like,'" Hannah said. "And 'don't fancy' means 'don't like.'"

"I'll be the snake carrier," Robinson said.

"All right then," Mrs. Timony said. "Cobra may stay for two days." Then she looked at Sam and me through her red eyeglasses and said, "After that he will be the guest of someone else. My suggestion is that you return him to nature."

"How do you know he's a him?" Clay asked.

"I'm guessing," Mrs. Timony said. "Now, on to the business of the day, which is writing a poem about your favorite thing."

"Back to snakes," I said.

10

REINVENTION NO. 2

Mr. Santalices had an after-school meeting with us. "Who has something to report?" he asked.

"I'm already finished," Marco said.

He held up two sparkling earrings as big as prunes. "They're for my mom," he said. "I made them out of crystals that were left over from when my dad tried to hang a chandelier on the dining room ceiling."

"That is a beautiful way to recycle," Mr. Santalices said. "But crystals hanging on ears is not that different from crystals hanging on chandeliers."

That made us all laugh like hoot owls.

"The judges are looking for something more unexpected—a reinvention that uses the crystals in a different way. For instance, if you designed an outdoor stove that held a crystal at an angle so that when sunshine passed through, it would start a small fire."

"Man alive, Marco," I said. "The next thing you know your mom's shoulders will be going up in smoke."

Marco looked terrorized until Mr. Santalices told him, "Your mom moves too much for that to happen but it is possible that the light going through the crystals will make rainbows on her shoulders."

"He's doing it again," Ashley said, and pointed at the front legs of my chair.

"Adam," Mr. Santalices said.

"Don't worry," I said. "I'm balancing my knees on the bottom of my desk for safety."

"Down, boy," he said to me.

To everybody else he said, "Any more ideas?"

"I'm making an exercise machine for cats," Pierra said. "I'm using my old skateboard and some kind of strong motor."

"My reinvention will save the environment," Kathleen said.

"All of it?" Mr. Santalices asked.

"I'd say so," she said.

"Robinson?" Mr. Santalices said.

"Mine will turn people into better dancers," she said.

"That will solve one of my problems," Mr. S said.

He called on Ashley.

"I'm not telling," she said. "Someone might steal my idea."

"Ashley," Mr. Santalices said. "We are here to help each other. One student's disaster can inspire another student's success. No one will swipe your invention."

"They'll see it when I win," Ashley said.

"Melonhead and I will tell ours," Sam said. "It's called Fight the Bite. Part One: Get a thousand bats."

"Why would anyone want a thousand bats?" Marisol asked.

"Because one bat can eat about six hundred mosquitoes in one hour," I said.

"Do they only eat at night?" Jonique asked.

"I think they have to digest in the day," Sam said.

"So if they eat for ten hours, one bat eats six thousand mosquitoes every night," she said. "One thousand bats would eat six million. Nobody has six million mosquitoes."

Jonique can multiply in her head.

"A lady mosquito lays hundreds of eggs a week," I said. "It's easy for a hundred to turn into six million."

Next, I went behind the supply closet door to make my fast changes for Part Two while Sam distracted everybody.

Then I popped out. Everybody laughed. Bart fell off his chair on purpose. He acted like it was because I looked so hilarious he couldn't control his body.

"You have black socks on your arms," Marisol said.

"Remember, great inventions can come from unlikely parts," Mr. Santalices said.

I could feel creeping redness on my cheeks. At

least no one could tell because the stocking leg I was wearing on my head made my face look tan. Also flat. Sam didn't have any way to hide his embarrassment.

"The Body Protector is excellent-O," Lucy Rose said. "Mosquitoes can't suck people's blood through socks."

Sometimes she comes up with a way to save us.

"What's with the wrapping-paper tube?" Pierra asked.

"It's a Carbon Dioxide Transporter," Sam said. "Mosquitoes are crazy about our breath."

"Stink-a-dink-a-doo," Robinson said. "How come?"

"They LOVE carbon dioxide so when you exhale out they fly near you. Then they bite you," I said. "But when you breathe through the Transporter your carbon dioxide comes out three feet away from your body."

"Adam and Sam, I congratulate you," Mr. S

said. "That is the kind of problem solving that, back in 1903, inspired Albert Parkhouse of the Timberlake Wire and Novelty Company to snip off a piece of wire and bend it."

"He invented bent wire?" Clayton asked.

"No," Mr. S said. "He invented the coat hanger."

"Really?" I said. "What was his problem?"

"Lots of employees. Not enough coat hooks," Mr. S said.

11

SNAKE SNACK

After school Jonique, Lucy Rose, and Hannah went to Madam and Pop's. They think the best time in life is doing fashion shows with Madam's clothes. Why they think it I do not know. Sam and I packed up our snake and followed them because we were starving. We left Cobra on the porch in case Madam was back from New Jersey.

We all helped Pop make blueberry smoothies. While the blender was blending, Lucy Rose told him, "I wrote a poem about the snake situation."

"Let's hear it," Pop said.

"A snake gets stuck if it eats honey.
It sticks to its ribs and sickens its tummy.
It can make a snake's nose runny.
But a starving reptile is not funny.
They'd buy mice if they had money."

Lucy Rose pointed at Sam and me.

"That is a first-rate poem," Pop said.

"Mrs. Washburn said it gave her the willies so I'll probably get a hundred percent on it," she said.

"How much do mice cost?" Pop asked us.

"They're bound to be expensive," Sam said. "Otherwise everybody would have them."

"Where will Cobra be living?" Pop asked.

"Mrs. Timony said to give him liberty," Hannah said.

"He's going to live at my house," Sam said. "My mom is reasonable about reptiles."

"I'm glad she agreed," Pop said.

"She didn't say yes yet because she doesn't know we have a snake," Sam said.

"But when we tell her she'll be ecstatic. Believe me," I said.

"Is ecstatic good?" Hannah asked.

"It's when you're overjoyed to pieces and bits," Lucy Rose said.

"Since Cobra's housing issues are settled, I'd like to contribute five dollars to the mouse fund," Pop said.

"Hail, Pop!" I said.

Sam and I tied the cardboard condo to Lucy Rose's skateboard, clipped Gumbo's old leash to the string, and gave Cobra a snake-thrilling ride to Pete's Pet Palace. That store has everything an animal could dream of owning.

I couldn't believe Pete's prices. "Mice are the deal of the century," I said. "Hardly anything costs three for a dollar."

Sam took the roof off the condo and introduced Cobra to the head of the snake department.

"We'll take fifteen mice," I said.

"I can sell you a bag of frozen mice," he said. "Just make sure you defrost before feeding. But if

you're going with live ones, don't buy more than two at a time. Cobra will only eat one every week."

"Which mice are more expensive?" I asked.

"Frozen," he said. "And a lot of moms won't give them freezer space."

"My mom wouldn't," I said. "She is overly anti-snake and even more anti-rodent."

"That is so weird," Sam said.

"My dad says we all have quirks," I said.

"Except for us," Sam said.

"We'll take the cheap, live ones," I said. "One to eat here and one to go."

We chose a teensy mouse. When Sam dropped it in the condo, Cobra made his body into a standing S and bit. Then he stretched his jaws and swallowed it whole. It was a little sad.

"That'll be sixty-six cents," the owner said. "Plus tax."

The mouse-to-go came in a white box with a wire handle like you get from Hunan on the Hill restaurant. The mouse was scratching inside.

"Swinging relaxes Julia," Sam said. "It probably works on mice, too."

I pulled the snakemobile while Sam swung and the scratching stopped.

Then I thought about my dad. "Do you think mice get carsick?" I asked.

"Maybe," Sam said. "But I never heard of a mouse throwing up."

"That's good."

When we got to Sam's we found Mrs. Alswang in the living room, walking around and around their green rug, trying to get Julia to fall asleep. She perked up when she saw us. "You brought my two favorite things," she said. "Shoes and Chinese food!"

"It's food," I said. "But not the Chinese kind."

"I'll bet your sweet mother sent it, Adam," Mrs. Alswang said. "She and I had a chat at Baking Divas and ever since I've been daydreaming about their fabulous chocolate bread pudding."

"It's even better that that," Sam said.

"Lemon cake with orange zest and buttercream frosting?" she guessed.

"Close your eyes, Mom," Sam said.

Mrs. Alswang did but she kept smiling and jiggling Julia, who was completely awake. "I am a woman in need of a treat," she said.

"Tweet," Julia said, and held out her hand.

Sam opened the Chinese box and held it under his mom's eyes. "You can look!" he said.

Mrs. Alswang jumped backwards and screamed, "Aaagghh!"

"Aah!" Julia laughed and tried to grab the mouse.

Sam pulled the box back.

"Tweet," Julia said, and held out both hands.

Mrs. Alswang looked dizzy. So did the mouse. "That was an awful trick," she said.

"Twikatweet," Julia said.

Sam got upset. "But you like mice, Mom," he said. "It was supposed to be a great surprise."

"I do like mice. I don't like finding one under my nose when I'm expecting a lovely dessert," she said.

Sam's head went down so far his chin touched his Washington Wizards sweatshirt. "I never thought you'd be the kind of mom who would pick bread pudding over a mouse," he said.

"You can't show up with a mouse without asking first," she said.

"I'm sorry," Sam said.

"If we ever thought that you wouldn't want a surprise mouse, we wouldn't have done it," I said. It's impossible to predict adults.

"Okay," Sam's mom said. "What's in the other box?" We did not answer.

Julia was chewing their mom's orange eyeglasses.

Mrs. Alswang smiled a tiny bit. "Is it a . . . hedgehog?"

"Hot dog," Julia said.

"An armadillo?" Mrs. Alswang asked.

"I'm a pillow," Julia said.

"Tell me," Mrs. Alswang said. "What is it?"

Sam made a joke of that. "A snake it is," he said.

"Naked is," Julia said.

Mrs. Alswang laughed and took off the box top.

"Get prepared," Sam said at the last second.

"Don't look," I said too late.

"Sam," Mrs. Alswang said. "Snakes also require permission."

"I just figured that out," Sam said.

"Okay," she said. "Your snake needs a better house. Get the fishbowl you used for the terrarium."

"You are my kind of mom," I said.

Sam pulled up ivy from the front yard and found sticks in the back. I made food and water dishes out of yogurt lids I got out of the trash.

Then we turned the snake condo into a mouse house. The mouse, who we decided not to name because he will just end up eaten, didn't pay attention to his new home, but he paid a lot to the Cheerios I dropped on his floor. When he ate one it looked like he was having a donut. Cobra looked comfortable in the old terrarium. As comfortable as anyone can be with a whole mouse in their stomach.

12

KNEE-DEEP IN WET DIAPERS

To make the weekend last longer I get up early. My mom does not. When she's asleep she wears a mask like the Lone Ranger's but without the eye-holes. She also wears a sleeping hat to keep her hair in order.

Since my dad is in Florida for two days and one night, I had to wake my mom up to ask if I could go to Sam's. Once I didn't and she thought I'd been stolen.

She pulled up a side of her mask and looked at me with one eyeball. "No swinging so high that you almost fly around the top bar," she said.

"Believe me," I said. "I have learned that lesson."

"No prying open a manhole cover to see what's under it," she said.

"I'm not curious about that anymore," I said.

"Okay. Remember that I love you and call when you get to Sam's," she said. "And bring his mom the box of donuts that's on our counter."

"She's kind of against dessert these days," I said. "But I'll eat them."

"Maybe Mrs. Alswang will offer you one," my mom said.

She was right. Probably because when Mrs. Alswang said, "How are you?" I said, "Starving."

"Star king," Julia said, and pointed at me.

Mrs. Alswang laughed. I made a kingly wave.

"Sam and his dad are at Eastern Market buying a honeydew melon," Mrs. Alswang said.

"Mel in," Julia said, and grabbed my hair.

"You know my name!" I said. "Smart baby!"

Sam's mom pointed at the yellow smears on her white sweater and said, "Would you mind watching Julia while I wash away the sweet potatoes she shared with me?"

"Sure," I said.

Mrs. Alswang plopped Julia on the rug and said, "I'll be upstairs."

When she was gone I said, "Julia, I have never been in charge of a baby before."

"Baby bee," Julia said.

"I'll start by picking you up," I told her. "Don't cry or anything."

I put my hands under her armpits and lifted her in the air. That made her laugh so I invented a game called Baby Elevator. When she looked like she might throw up, I sat down on the sofa fast and put her on my knees. Then I made up a song about giant underwear. She clapped for it. When she started examining my face I said, "If you stop turning my eyelids inside out I'll show you something great."

I carried her to Sam's room and said, "Do you want to touch the snake?"

"Snack," Julia said. "Mine snack."

"No. The mouse is the snake snack," I said. "Joe's O's are the mouse snack." I let her drop some cereal into the mouse house.

Julia squealed with excitement. The mouse ran in circles. Probably it had never been in a cereal avalanche before.

Sam and his dad came home with the melon plus red tulips for Mrs. Alswang and bagels for Julia's new teeth.

"I had no idea you were so good with babies," Mr. Alswang said.

"Me either," I told him. "I also had no idea they are so heavy."

"She must have a full diaper," he said. "Julia herself is a lightweight."

"You can have her back now," I said.

Mr. Alswang changed her diaper one-handed. Then he wadded up the old one and tossed it into the trash. "I'll bet that diaper weighs four pounds," he said.

"How could it?" I said. "It's not that big."

"Diapers have super-absorbent stuff inside," he said.

I looked at Sam. I could tell we were thinking alike.

"See you later," Sam said, and we ran upstairs.

"First we have to feed Cobra," I reminded him. "The lump from last week's mouse is gone."

Since I was feeling attached to the mouse with no name, I turned backwards after we dropped it in the bowl. "I'm glad it got one last snack," I said. When I looked again the only thing to see was a lumpy snake.

While Cobra was digesting, we got a stack of clean diapers from Julia's room and filled the toothbrush cup with water. "Our testing area will be the floor in my room," Sam said.

After I poured the water on a diaper and saw it disappear we took turns refilling and pouring. Once we got the answer, we did the whole experiment two more times, to be sure. Then I wrote in our log:

The diapers didn't leak until cup number 11. We cut them open. They were full of mush. Sam cut open a dry diaper. White crystals were inside. It takes 29 diapers to get enough crystals to fill half of Mrs. Alswang's coffee mug. We triple-checked that, too.

You would think Mrs. Alswang would be thrilled to have inventors in the house. Wrong!

"Whad-I-do?" Sam asked her.

When she told him he said, "How was I supposed to know?"

"Diapers don't look expensive," I said.

"It was for research," Sam said.

"I'm sorry," I said.

Lately those are my two most popular words.

13

THE SHORTCUT

Sam came over for Cap'n Crunch. I made it with ginger ale instead of milk. "It's unlimited," I said. "Have all you want."

"Too bad we're not in a cooking contest," Sam said. "This recipe would win."

When we were done, we walked to Grubb's drugstore to buy Skittles. "Here's another one of my famous recipes," I told him. "Pour the whole bag in your mouth at once and chew. It makes tutti-frutti."

"Another masterpiece," Sam said.

I pulled two tennis balls out of my cargo pocket so we could bounce them off the side of the drugstore while we thought about what we could rein-vent.

"How about a solar egg fryer?" Sam said.

"If it rained we'd be out of luck, Chuck," I said. "But what about vegetarian snake food? Our motto could be: Be Nice, Save Mice!"

"Not a winning plan, Dan," Sam said. "Maybe we could use the spring from our screen door to make a tennis ball shooter?"

"Already invented," I told him. "In Florida there's a rich lady that has one at her house."

We were in the middle of thinking when Eddie the pharmacist came outside and said, "Boys, the sound of balls hitting the wall is driving me insane."

"Oops. I never thought about that," I said. "To me plunking is a restful noise."

We went across the street to Johnny and Joon's store to ask if it would bother them and also to buy a pack of Hostess Sno-Balls.

"Sugar fuels our brains," I told Johnny. He watched us peel the coconut marshmallow igloos off the cake insides. Then we each bit a hole near

the edge of the igloo. "Watch this," I said. "We press the skinny part under our noses like a mustache. Then we stretch the rest over our chins. Presto! A stick-on pink goatee."

Joon got his camera from under the counter. "That is a crazy look," he said. "I'm going to hang your picture on our bulletin board."

"Be prepared," I said. "A lot of people will recognize me from when I was on TV."

Sam and I walked and talked in front of Eastern Market but it's hard to dream up a reinvention when you're a main attraction. Mrs. Hackett said,

"I almost didn't recognize you boys with those handsome beards." Mrs. Bonora thought I had a rash. When we stopped off at the Baking Divas, Mrs. McBee said, "Scat before you scare away my customers." But before we did she asked if we would like to have the tuna sandwich Jonique left in the refrigerator.

"No, thanks," I said. "We're only eating small things so our goatees won't get shabby."

She filled up a little bag, gave it to us and said, "Behave yourselves." We took it to the Supreme Court and sat on a marble step for a peanut and raisin picnic. It was not enough food. Luckily, I had a pocketful of Artificially Flavored Limited Edition Sparkling Green Apple Jinx cereal.

Most tourists stared at us but a lady who was wearing a shirt covered with pictures of cats sat down next to me. She didn't notice our beards. She just said, "My dogs are killing me."

"That's the only pet I don't want," I told her. "A killer dog."

"It's an expression," she said. "It means my feet

hurt. I'm from Dallas, Texas. We tend to drive there. Here I walk. All the way from the White House. Uphill."

"A good reinvention would be shoe-shaped pillows," I said.

"I'd buy a pair," she said.

I was asking her if she knew any Dallas Cowboys or any of the horse-riding kind when Sam socked my shoulder and said, "It's four-fifty-five!"

"Whoa, buddy! We're in trouble now," I said. "Start running!"

"Hope your feet feel better," Sam called back to the lady.

"Take the shortcut, Chicken Butt," I yelled to Sam, not the lady.

My mom says any discussion that has to do with chicken butts is vile and worse than talking about regular butts. I cannot agree with her.

Thanks to our shortcut, I got home at 5:16, which was only sixteen minutes too late. My mom was waiting on the steps with her arms folded in that unpleasant way.

"I have three words for you," she said.

"I love you?" I asked her.

"I do love you, of course," she said. "But these three words are: Dr. Bowers called."

"He did?" I asked.

"I think you know what I'm going to say," she said.

"I don't know exactly," I said.

"Dr. Bowers said he was in the middle of fitting a patient for false teeth when he looked up and saw a boy JUMPING over his skylight," she said. "Can you explain that?"

Probably a lot of people take that shortcut.

"What did he look like?" I asked.

"Dr. Bowers said he saw your face, which he insisted was covered with some sort of pink

fungus," she said. "I told him he had the wrong boy because mine does not have a fungus."

"You're right. I don't," I said. I did not say that my goatee came off when it stuck to a rosebush so I ate it. This was no time to bring up the thought of germs.

"Dr. Bowers said he doesn't know much about fungi but he did recognize your navy blue jacket with one sleeve splattered with yellow paint. He also mentioned your homemade haircut," she said. "But the big giveaway was that you have been to see him three times in the past two months."

"He sure did a great job fixing my teeth after they hit the jungle gym," I said. "You can't even tell where they were busted."

My mom ignored that compliment.

"He said Sam was with you," she said.

Right then a taxicab stopped in front of our house and my dad got out. There were two bad signs about that. The first was that he only takes taxis when it's serious. The second was that the Capitol dome light was on.

"It seems like I always get in trouble when Congress is voting," I told him.

"Sport," my dad said. "What were you doing on the roof?"

"Being responsible," I said.

"How is roof-walking responsible?" he asked.

"Roof-RUNNING," my mom said.

"Remember, last time you said 'No excuses.' I had to take the shortcut so I'd get home on time."

"How is the roof quicker than the sidewalk?" he asked.

"I don't know," I said. "It just is. Sam and I have timed it lots of times."

That was not a good answer.

"I mean, that's a great thing about row houses," I explained. "Since the roofs are attached you can run for a block without having to slow down because there are no red lights or people or strollers or dogs in the way."

My mom sucked in air.

"Don't worry," I said. "We NEVER go near the edge. Not even when someone dares us."

"How did you get on the roof?" my mom asked.

"We climbed up the apartment building fire escape," I said in a mumbling voice.

"How did you get down?" she asked.

"The Walkers' house is the last tall one so we jump down onto the Pulanskis' roof," I said. "The triangle thing that holds up their rosebushes makes a great ladder to the ground. And don't worry, it's sturdy."

"You have been JUMPING off the Walkers' roof?" my mom said. Her voice was squeaking.

"It's a short jump," I said.

My dad pulled off his tie and undid the top button of his shirt. "Let's finish this talk inside," he said.

Since everything in our living room is white, I keep clear of it. But our living room is always where we go for serious family talks. I sat on the floor by the fireplace. My dad used the chair that's for company.

My mom sat on the sofa and held her forehead. "ALL I could think was that you could have FALLEN straight through the skylight and landed on the examining chair," she said. "My ONLY comfort was knowing that the patient would have broken your fall but, Adam, YOU could have BROKEN your LEGS."

"I never thought of that," I said.

"Sport," my dad said, "what made you think it was okay to get on any roof?"

"I'm allowed on Pop and Madam's breezeway roof," I said.

"It has a fence on the sides," my dad said.

"Oh," I said.

"After the tree incident we agreed you wouldn't climb to any new heights," he said.

"You said don't climb any TREES," I said. "And I haven't, even when Bart Bigelow said he'd pay me a dollar eighty-six to reenact getting stuck."

"Did you think that our neighbors don't want you and Sam running around on their roofs?" he asked.

"No," I said. "I never thought that."

"Adam, you have to be more considerate," my mom said. "If I heard footsteps on our roof it would chill me to my bones."

"Oh," I said.

"What bothers me most is that you have taken this shortcut several times but you never mentioned it to me or Mom," my dad said. "I think that's because you thought your shortcut wouldn't fly with us."

"Don't say 'fly' in front of Adam," my mom said.

"I didn't tell because of Mom's touchy nerves," I said.

"What makes you think I have touchy nerves?" she asked.

I was going to say Jonique but I stopped myself. Instead I said, "When Lucy Rose told the entire neighborhood that Mrs. Mannix was having a baby, Lucy Rose's mom said, 'You don't have to tell everybody everything.' "

"You shouldn't tell other people's private business," my dad said. "You should tell your parents what you are up to, ideally when you are in the planning stage. Got it?"

"Got it," I said. "The problem is I don't always plan. A lot of times I just do."

"I'm going to have to let Sam's parents know what happened," my mom said.

"I do not agree that parents have to tell each other everything," I said.

After dinner with no dessert, my mom called and, just like I predicted, Mrs. Alswang was unhappy. My dad walked me over to apologize to Dr. Bowers. That was embarrassing. Especially since I wasn't sure he was over the dirt-clump-throwing incident. Even though it was an accident and I had no way of knowing what a clump can do when it hits a dentist.

14

FALLING BEHIND

Mr. Santalices came to our classroom after recess. *"Hola, amigos,"* he said. "Do I smell success?"

"You smell my Supersonic Tonic," Amir said. "It makes bad medicine taste better and gives you energy."

"What are the ingredients?" Mr. S asked.

"Maple syrup and chocolate sauce mixed with butter, mint leaves, one drop of Tabasco sauce, and black Jelly Bellys," Amir said.

"All that sugar would give you energy and the combination of ingredients would cover up some of the nastiest flavors," Mr. Santalices said. "Have you found a taste tester?"

"I put Supersonic Tonic in my dad's Bromo Seltzer," Amir said.

"How'd that go?"

"His stomach was still upset and he was too," Amir said. "But it did cover up the medicine taste."

"I'm not sure the judges will think mixing food together is enough of a reinvention to win," Mr. S said.

"That's not fair," Amir said.

"Yes it is," Ashley told him.

I think she said that to bug Amir.

"Ashley," Mr. Santalices said. "Are you ready to tell us what you've been working on?"

"I am not," she said.

"How about you, Lucy Rose?"

"I used my Gimp that I had left over from lanyard making and wove it through the fence, which took about seventy-seven thousand hours, and I tied bells all over it so that escaping dog would stay away. But Rex chewed right through it."

"You need to try again," Mr. S said.

"I already did. Since he is a chicken of a dog who is scared of water, I put all of Madam's lasagna pans and pie plates in front of the fence and flooded them with the hose. I was right. He wouldn't walk in water. He drank all of it out of one pan and walked across it and out and I had to run my legs off to catch him. Now I have nothing but fatigue, which is the exact same as being exhausted to death."

"Who can help Lucy Rose?" Mr. S asked.

"Make an elastic leash," Pierra said. "Then Rex can run in the yard but can't stretch through the fence."

"I tied my hair bands into a long line and hooked one end to the railing and the other end to Rex's collar," Lucy Rose said. "But he ran in circles and got utterly tangled in Madam's rosebushes and pink petals fell all over him, which made him get anxiety and bark like mad and made Madam feel like she was frustrated on account of she was going to cut those roses and bring them to her friend that's in the hospital for having bunions on her feet, whatever they are. I mean bunions. I know what feet are, of course. I was scratched to pieces and bits rescuing that dog."

"Yikes," Pierra said.

"Sam and Adam, how are you coming along?" Mr. Santalices asked.

"We reinvented a way to keep the pacifier in my baby sister's mouth because she keeps spitting it out and crying until I pick it up and give it back," Sam said.

"I can see how that would be useful," Mr. S said.

"We had to cancel it because my mom says we'll be in serious trouble if we ever put tape on Julia's face again," Sam said. "Now Melonhead and I decided that whatever it is, we're doing it with acid."

"Very carefully and without involving your sister, I hope," Mr. Santalices said.

"We're using the kind of acid that comes in car batteries," I said.

"No, you're not," Mr. S said. "It's too strong. Try a mild acid, the kind you can eat."

"I would never eat acid," Sam said.

"You do it all the time," Mr. S said. "Lemons, limes, and grapefruit all contain acid. So does the vinegar we put in salad dressing."

"We'll think of another idea," I said.

"Good," Mr. S said. "You're falling behind." That was the exact second my chair tipped backwards with me on it.

"Your falling behind just hit the floor," Bart yelled.

Everybody laughed.

"Do you need to go to the health room?" Mr. S asked me.

"No," I said. There are some situations that get talked about forever. I'm sure going to the nurse for a broken butt is one of them.

"Now is the time for everyone else to start refining your reinventions," Mr. Santalices said.

"Huh?" Bart said.

"Refining is like making puny changes so they work better and don't have glitches," Lucy Rose said. "It's my Word of the Day."

15

NAKED FLIES

To save time, I ate my Wild Mountain Burst flavored Pop-Tart raw while I put on my shoes and my dad flipped sausages.

I have been wanting to tell him about Cobra ever since we found him but I haven't, because first my mom was with us, and then the skylight situation happened. Now that we were alone I said, "We got a snake!"

"Nuts!" my dad said. "I didn't see that coming!"

"Most people couldn't," I said. "It was raining."

"Hot grease doesn't rain so much as it splatters," my dad said. "Mostly on my tie."

"Are you listening?" I asked.

"Sorry, sport," he said. "Start over."

"I am trying to tell you what happened to Sam and me in Seward Square," I said.

"What happened?" my mom said. "Did someone scare you? Was it a bully?"

I hadn't heard her come in so for a second my mind was empty. Then I said, "No one scared us, Mom. We slid on mud, that's all."

"Next time, look where you are going so you can walk around the mud," she said. "Otherwise you could break your neck."

"I've got to go," I said, and dumped four sausages and Cap'n Crunch in my coat pocket for later. "I'm meeting Sam at Jimmy T's restaurant." I left out that we were getting a bagel with strawberry jelly to eat on the walk to school.

I was spinning on a counter stool when Sam came. "In my mind I'm inventing a way to power the Ts' grill with chandelier crystals," I said.

"Neato, Cheeto," Sam said. "But we can't stay. My mom and dad want to talk to us."

Those are words I hate to hear. "What did we do?" I asked.

Sam pushed his shoulders up to his ears. "I can't think of anything," he said.

"Me either," I said. "But a lot of times when I can't think of why I'd need talking to, it turns out that I do."

We waited for the traffic to turn, then ran across the street and through his front door. "I'm back with Melonhead!" Sam hollered.

"We're in the kitchen," Mrs. Alswang said.

His mom and dad were eating granola with yogurt. Julia had olives stuck on all her fingers. "Help yourself to granola," his dad said. "Or olives."

I did. Sam didn't.

"What's the talk about?" Sam asked them.

"At five o'clock this morning Julia crawled into our bed and snuggled in between us," Sam's mom said. "I was too sleepy to open my eyes but I patted her head and said, 'Hello.' Then Julia patted my nose and said, 'Naked flies.' I took a look and saw that she was tossing a piece of rope in the air. But when I put on my glasses I realized that the rope was a snake."

"Uh-oh," Sam said. "Snake, it flies."

"I woke up to a big scream and little giggles," Sam's dad said. "But before we could gather our wits, Cobra landed. He went for cover under our covers. He wiggled over my ankle and inside the leg of my pajama pants and headed north to my thigh, which, let me tell you, is a ticklish situation."

Sam's eyes popped forward. "Is he still in your pants?" he asked.

"Ants," Julia said.

"No ants," Mr. Alswang told her.

Then he told us, "I don't like having any living creature in my pants except for myself."

Sam's mom said, "We found a soggy bagel in the terrarium. Cobra's yogurt lid was in the hall and sticks were floating in the toilet. It seems Julia carried Cobra around the house before she brought him into our bed."

"She's a smart baby," I said so Mrs. Alswang would see the good. "Creative, too."

"Where is Cobra now?" Sam asked.

"He's back in his bowl," Mr. Alswang said.

"Whew," I said. "I was afraid you lost him."

"He's safe," Sam's mom said. "But we are retiring from our job as snake keepers."

"NO!" Sam said. "I BEG of you, PLEASE can he stay? I PROMISE he'll never get in Dad's pants again."

"We'll put him up high," I said.

"Sorry, boys," Sam's dad said. "We'll reconsider snake owning when Julia is older. But now it's time for Cobra to be returned to the wilds of Capitol Hill."

"Can we at least wait until after school so we have time to say goodbye?" Sam asked.

"That sounds fair," his mom said.

At school I was squirming so much that Mrs. Timony asked me if I needed to go to the nurse. I never turn down a visit to the health room but today I did because all I could concentrate on was finding a home for Cobra. I thought so hard that I got 5 × 3 wrong.

Pop says Lucy Rose is a natural-born problem fixer so at lunch Sam and I had a talk with her. "Sorry," she said. "Cobra can't live at my house. Even though I'm more of a dog person than a snake person, I would go for it out of friendship but my mom would utterly not."

After school we walked to Baking Divas and I said, "Mrs. McBee, I need a good home for a good snake."

"Not my home," she said.

"Snakes aren't messy," Jonique told her mom.

"Or loud," Lucy Rose said. "Reptiles are silent as anything. Zippy but quiet, with the kind of personalities that are nothing but delightful. I'd say that after you are living with that snake for fifty-one minutes, you'll be so wild for him that you'll want five or six more."

"That snake could sweep the porch and polish my shoes. I still wouldn't have it in my house," Mrs. McBee said.

We were sitting under the outside roof at Eastern Market, licking the raspberry jam off the day-old cookies we got for free because we're Jonique's good friends, when Lucy Rose clobbered my arm with her lunch box and said, "I have a D-double D-vine idea."

I did my dance of triumph. "I knew you'd come up with one."

"Cobra can live at your house!" she said.

Sometimes I give that girl too much credit.

But Sam read her mind. "What if your mom didn't know?" he said. "With all the experiments and collections and junk and books in your room, Cobra can blend in the crowd of stuff. Your mom will never spot him."

"That could work!" I said. "My mom calls my room revolting. She won't go in most of the time."

"You should make it ultra-revolting," Lucy Rose said. "For extra added protection."

"Hey!" I said. "Remember that leaky aquarium at Mr. Neenobber's yard sale? I could use it for Cobra."

"I can't believe I said it was a waste of allowance," Sam said.

"One question," Jonique said. "Isn't sneaking a snake almost like lying about a snake?"

"Not at all," I said. "Because it's lifesaving. That's an allowable exception."

"When you're a city snake your life is overrun

with dangers," Lucy Rose said. "Cobra could get squished by a car or fall in a sewer and not know how to swim."

"He could freeze," Sam said. "Or be snake-napped."

"He might crawl into someone else's pants," Lucy Rose said. "And that person could get on the subway. The next thing you know, Cobra would get off at the Shady Grove Metro stop and he'd be lost in the extreme and scared out of his snake skin."

"Pop says you have to do the right thing, even when it's unpopular," I said.

"Snakes are very unpopular with your mom," Sam said.

"Face it," Jonique said. "We are the only ones who can save him."

We made our deal and went straight to Pete's. Jonique gave us thirty-four cents so we could afford a new mouse. Then we went to Sam's. I put Cobra in my pocket. Lucy Rose carried the new Chinese carton like it was a purse and she talked so much that she drowned out the mouse scratching. Then we went to my house.

"Remember to take off your shoes by the door," I said. "My mother thinks they carry dirt."

I was one-quarter of the way up the steps with a pocketful of snake and the mouse in a box stuffed under my T-shirt, when my mom came up from the laundry room.

"Hello, kids!" she said. "Anyone want cookies?"

"I'll be down in a sec," I said, running up the steps two at a time.

"Are you okay?" my mom asked.

"Completely," I said, and ran to my room.

I dusted out the aquarium with yesterday's socks and plunked Cobra in the corner with a few dull pencils for climbing. Then I ran to my mom's closet, took her flip-flops out of their plastic box, raced back to my room, and dumped the mouse in the box. "This will be like living in a glass house," I told it. "Anywhere you look you'll have a view."

When I got to the

top of the steps my mom was more than halfway up. "I was wondering what happened to you," she said.

"Nothing," I said. "But I'm starving."

In the kitchen Mint Milanos were on plates and milk was in plastic cups. "Sit at the table," my mom said. "And remember to use your napkins."

I love the feeling of having a pet living in my house. Two pets, actually, even though as soon as Cobra has his next lunch, I'll be back to one.

16

ANOTHER FINE IDEA

Sam and I were in the alley throwing rocks at Mrs. Young's trash can. "Ten extra points for the person who makes it tip over," Sam said.

My rock missed and bounced off their fence. "So far no parent suspects that there are pets in my room," I said. "My snake-owning dream has finally come true."

"One of my dreams is to get a cast," Sam said.

"On your arm or leg?" I asked.

"Doesn't matter," he said. "I just don't want the bone breaking to hurt too much."

"Remember when Jimmy Conroy broke his arm at the end-of-school picnic? Kids in his class said his bone poked through his skin and flew across the playground," I said.

"That had to hurt," Sam said.

"The bone flying part might be a rumor," I said.

"Here's a great reinvention!" Sam said. "We can invent a cast that kids could put on whenever they want without having to break their bones."

"We could cut the zipper off my sweatshirt so it can come off whenever we want," I said.

"And I'll tear off the inside pocket from my jeans and we can glue it on the inside for a hiding place for money," Sam said.

"Brilliant! Like a portable safe!" I said.

"Eddie knows all about busted bones," Sam said. "We should ask him for tips."

I pedaled my bike and Sam sat on the handlebars and, since he was blocking my view, told me when to swerve. At Grubb's we had to wait by Pickup while Eddie told Mr. West about athlete's foot cream even though Mr. West is no athlete. Believe me.

"In the old days, before casts came in colors, the docs used gauze covered with plaster of Paris,"

Eddie told us. "They would dip it in water and wrap it around the break. The cast would harden and, over time, the bone would heal."

"Do you sell plaster from Paris?" I asked.

"I don't," Eddie said. "But art stores sell sheets of plaster-covered fabric. Artists use it to make statues but as far as I can tell it's the same stuff."

We got to Innervision when it was closing. Even with Sam's allowance and my snack money, we didn't have enough. Luckily, when Miss Joanne heard it was for school she said we could bring her $1.07 tomorrow.

We rode like a tornado to Sam's and locked ourselves in the upstairs bathroom. Since two safes are better than one, Sam cut the front pockets out of his jeans and I clipped the zipper off my sweatshirt with Mrs. Alswang's fingernail scissors. Since it was Sam's dream, he got to be the patient. "We'll cut it into strips and put it on your arm," I told him. "When it gets a little hard, I'll cut the cast on the back so it will be removable where no one can see."

"We can glue the zipper to the cut edges," Sam said. "That way, E-Z on, E-Z off."

"You're smart, Fart," I said.

That rhyme is our all-time favorite.

I soaked the first strip in hot water for fifteen seconds and wound it around Sam's hand seven times.

"How does it feel?" I asked.

"Hot," he said. "But in a good way."

"Bend your elbow," I said, so he'd look good in a sling.

It only took half our supply to get up to his armpit. I smoothed the ridges out with my hands.

"When I grow up, if I can't get a job being an inventor, I'll just be a doctor instead," I said.

"Good thinkin', Lincoln," he said.

"Hey!" I said. "Look at the floor. The stuff sheds. The green tiles look like they're covered with snow."

I used a wet towel to mop up the plaster dust. Sam sat in the tub to protect his cast.

"The floor looks brand-new," he said.

That was before we knew the trickiness of plaster.

"I think the water makes plaster turn into liquid that looks invisible. Then it dries and looks like the floor was washed with white paint," I said.

I used every towel and washcloth plus all the clothes in the hamper and all the toilet paper on the roll but every time I remopped, the white grew.

"Remember in *The Cat in the Hat*, when pink covers the walls and the dress and everything in sight?" Sam said. "I used to think that was impossible."

With his free arm he sprayed the floor with mildew cleaner and Pledge that we found under the sink. I poured a big puddle of Mop & Glo wax and scrubbed with a pink fluff thing that turned out to be for washing Mrs. Alswang's legs. The floor was a worse wreck than before.

Sam said the dreaded words: "We'd better tell my mom."

"First we have to cut off your cast," I said. "Otherwise, she could panic."

If it hadn't been for the floor emergency I'm sure we would have noticed how fast that cast stuff dries. "It's thicker than I thought it would be," Sam said.

"Harder, too," I said. "It won't cut."

I took off my raggedy-edged Orange You Glad You're in Florida? sweatshirt and tossed it to Sam. "Put it on so your mom can't see your arm," I said. "We'll get the cast off after we figure out the floor."

Mrs. Alswang was not calm.

"WHAT exploded in this bathroom?" she said.

Julia was thrilled.

"Ess-plo!" she yelled. "Ess-plo ded bafoom!"

"It's only plaster dust," Sam said.

"Passed her," Julia said, and clapped.

"It's a plaster disaster," his mom said.

"Passed her DIS asser," Julia sang.

"I tried to scrub it," I said.

"Rub it," Julia said, and smeared her hands on the floor.

"Everybody out!" Mrs. Alswang said. "Sam, mind your sister. Adam, go home."

"I'm sorry," I said. "I wish we had invented that Sweep the Nation machine."

Thinking that she was going to call my parents made me so nervous that I could only eat three pieces of meat loaf. But after two hours passed I relaxed. That was when the phone rang. "Ralph is at the hospital with Sam," Mrs. Alswang told my dad. "Julia and I are at home waiting for the plumber."

Who knew that when plaster from Paris goes down the drain it gets hard inside the pipes? I didn't. Believe me. Another thing I never knew is that the only way to get a cast off is with a special saw.

My dad told Sam's mom that he'd pay for half the plumber and half the hospital. Then he told me that I shouldn't think about getting any allowance until I'm eleven.

17

WHO KNEW THIS COULD HAPPEN?
NOT ME

Sam brought both halves of his cast to school so we could all try them on. That was fun. After school my dad came home early so we could talk some more about my personal responsibility. That was not.

We discussed while my mom cooked chicken. Then my mom talked about it while we ate the chicken. The topic made me feel like laying my head on my plate and having a snooze. That happens when I get brain overload. But all of a sudden I felt like my thoughts were zinging, and my eyes felt like they were jumping out of my skull. "It looks like the message is finally sinking in," my mom told my dad. "Adam looks like he's in shock."

"Ha-ha," I said.

I tried to stop looking at the oil painting that used to be in the guest room until the artist got famous and my mom put a curly gold frame on it and hung it in the dining room.

"Do you see the problem, sport?" my dad said.

"I see it," I said. It felt like my tonsils were taking up my whole throat.

Behind my mom, in one of the curliest parts of the golden frame, was my mouse.

"Good," my dad said. "We have to think of the consequences before we act."

"I sure didn't this time," I said.

"Think about them before you get on the roof," he said. "Before you wrap your friend in plaster-covered gauze."

Miracle! My dad wasn't talking about the mouse. He hadn't even seen it. I was the only one who had and I couldn't take my eyes off it. That was a mistake because my staring made my mom turn around and look.

"Are you developing an interest in art?" she asked.

"Yes, I am!" I said.

To distract her I ran into the living room and snatched a silver frame off the top of the piano. "I think this picture is excellent," I said.

"Adam," my mom said. "As much as I love my parents, I don't think their photo is considered art."

"I do," I said. "Let's all sit down on the sofa and look at it."

"Let's return to the table for mint ice cream," my mom said.

"I'm too stuffed to eat it," I said.

"Sport," my dad said. "What is going on here?"

"What do you mean by going on?" I asked.

"You are never too full for dessert," he said.

"I must be mature now. I'm completely out of stomach space," I said. "How about you guys relax in here? I'll clear the table."

"That is mature," my dad said.

"And thoughtful," my mom said. "But no, thank you, Adam. You might drop a plate and cut yourself."

"It will give me personal responsibility," I said.

"He has to learn sometime," my dad said.

"He's only nine," my mom said.

"Clear the table, sport," my dad said. "Carefully."

Then he patted a couch pillow and said, "Come sit with me, Betty."

"I'll shut the pocket doors for your privacy," I said.

The second they were out of my sight, I climbed on top of the sideboard and searched the picture frame. No mouse. I looked inside the light that shines on the valuable painting. I was glad I didn't find him there because forty watts might fry a mouse.

I didn't think that tiny rodent could scramble up to the big light over the table but I never thought it could get in a picture frame, either. I stepped off the sideboard onto my chair and *very* carefully stepped over my dad's plate, to get to the middle of the table. One foot was on one side of a bowl and the other foot was on the other side. I tipped the tan glass that covers the lightbulbs.

That way, if the mouse was in it, he'd have a soft landing in the potatoes.

The sharpest voice I ever heard said, "WHAT are YOU doing?"

Shock made me yank my hands off the light. That made it swing away from me. Then it swung back and bonked me in the forehead, which made me lose my balance and step on the platter. Out of the edge of my eye, I saw something swoosh through the air. It landed in my mom's hairdo.

"What is this?" My mom grabbed it and shrieked. I looked at her hand. That was the exact moment that I knew my childhood was going to be troubled forever.

"Creamed spinach," I said. Then I laughed because I was so glad it wasn't the mouse.

"This is not funny," my mom said.

"Accidents happen," my dad said.

"I don't understand how this one happened," she said.

"I believe I stepped on the fork and the spinach catapulted," I said.

"Why are you standing on the table?" she asked.

I was about to confess about the runaway mouse when my dad said, "There's no telling what inspired it, Betty. Let's accept it and move on."

Then he said: "Adam, take your foot out of the mashed potatoes. Put the tablecloth in the laundry room." His voice was soft with Mom but not with me.

I did a great job clearing the table with hardly any thanks from my parents.

18

ANOTHER THING THAT SEEMED LIKE A GOOD IDEA

After school, I put on the Body Protector and stomped around the backyard. Sam stomped without one. This was triply brilliant. For one, since the table incident I am not allowed to go roaming. For two, since my mom was still steaming, the yard was better than the house. For three, she couldn't hear our conversation.

"The mouse has been on the loose for twenty hours," I said.

"It will come back when it gets hungry," Sam said. "Maybe faster if we add an Oreo to its Cocoa Puffs."

When one hour was up I wrote in our log:

Melonhead has 2 mosquito bites and a lot of sweat. Sam has 6 bites but not so much sweat. We estimate that the Protector works 2/3 of the time. A snafu is that it's hot to wear in spring and summer and there are no mosquitoes in the winter.

Sam wrote:

Not a total flop.

"Why did you boys purposely tempt mosquitoes?" my mom asked while she painted our bites with sticky pink lotion that's supposed to take itches away. It doesn't work.

"Reinventors have to test their reinventions," I said.

"Do they have to retest their mother's patience?" she asked.

"They don't mean to," I told her. My patience was fine but my mind was going nutty. Every time anything moved I thought it was the mouse.

We used up the good Band-Aids last week

when I scuffed my elbows while I was practicing stomach crawling in case I'm ever in the army. Now I was covered with Elmo and Cookie Monster. They were left over from when I was a kid. Sam peeled his off on the walk home.

Luckily my parents had to go to a reception for the Florida orange growers who were visiting Washington, D.C.

"Stay out as long as you can," I told them.

Julianne Meany was my babysitter. She should be named Julianne Nicey. She is not a person who falls apart when a boy gets in a situation with a mouse.

"Mice like kitchens," she said.

"Oh, no!" I said. "That's my mom's main room."

"Got a flashlight?" Julianne asked.

"Penlight, regular, the kind that you wind and never needs batteries, or the big emergency one?" I asked. "I have all of those in my room."

"This is an emergency so get that one," she said. "And bring the penlight so we can look in nooks. Mice enjoy nooks."

Julianne looked first. "This is the only fridge I

ever saw that doesn't have dust balls under it," she said.

"I'll climb on top and look behind it," I said.

"I'll get you a chair," she said.

"That's okay," I said. "I've been climbing refrigerators since I was three and a half."

We had no good luck with that or with the dishwasher or the bread box.

Julianne had to take a break to have a long talk on the phone about ninth grade with someone who I think is her boyfriend. That was when I was struck with the idea. I ran upstairs to my room and unwound the string from the automatic door shutter I built last summer. I didn't mind taking it apart. It turned out to be more of an automatic door creaker than a shutter.

I tied the string around Cobra's stomach and held him so we were snake eyeballs to boy eyeball.

"Snake," I said, "I am depending on you. If you are as good a hunter as Mrs. Timony said, you'll hunt down your dinner but fast."

I held his string and put him on the kitchen floor. "Lead the way," I said.

Cobra headed for a cabinet. I followed. "Humans use two hundred muscles to take one step," I told him. "I wonder how many muscles you use per slither?"

He must have wanted to show me because he zigzagged himself right out of the string and under the stove. He was about as fast as the speed of sound.

Julianne found me with my head on the floor. "I can only see with one eye because the space under the oven is not even as high as one Pez candy," I said. "And now I have double trouble."

"What's the problem?" Julianne asked.

"Snakes have no hips," I said. "Or shoulders. And Cobra's last mouse was digested. I wish I'd realized that it takes some wider parts to keep a snake on a leash."

Julianne sat on the floor and pulled up her knees so her chin could have a place to rest. "Getting the snake to track the mouse wasn't a bad idea," she said.

That made me feel smarter. "How can I track both of them?" I asked.

"I don't know," Julianne said.

I felt worse again.

Then she said, "If you can't find them, chances are your mom won't either."

Just like that, my hope returned.

"You should tell your dad there are critters on the loose," she said. "Get in bed. I'll tell your dad that you want him to come and say good night when he gets home."

That was going to be a hard job considering I hadn't even gotten to tell him I was part owner of a snake.

19
A CLUE

When I woke up there was a Post-it note stuck to my forehead. It said, "Sport, I came to see you but you were asleep. I had to get to the office early this morning but we'll have time together tonight."

I put on yesterday's pants and socks that were sticking out from under my bed and my Florida Gators shirt. My mom is a teeth-brushing fanatic who thinks it's a disaster if you even skip one day but I had to see if anything was creeping around the kitchen. Luckily, my mom was the only one.

"Good morning, sweetheart," she said.

"Hi there," I said in a cheerful way.

"Are you looking for something?" she said.

"Breakfast," I said. "Only breakfast. Nothing else. At all."

"I'll fix your cereal while you're changing out of those dirty clothes," she said.

"I only wore them one time," I said.

"I can smell them from here," she said.

"You're very observant," I said. "That's a skill every scientist needs."

Then I had a terrible thought. "Don't fix me anything!" I said. "I'm old enough to fix my own!"

"Okay, but I'll pour the milk," she said.

"Back in a flash," I said.

I ran downstairs and put on the clothes that were on top of my clean laundry pile. When I got back, my mom's fingers were a millimeter from the cabinet knob.

I slipped my hand under hers. "I got it!" I said.

"Okay," she said. "I'll go fix the coffee."

The Frankenberry box was my first clue. The corner was chewed. Next to it was a stack of fake berries and tan Frankens. "I'm in the mood for Lucky Charms," I said.

"I thought you were tired of them," she said.

"All of a sudden I love them again."

I looked before I poured. "Nothing but cereal and delicious marshmallow surprises," I said.

"What else were you expecting?" she said.

I made a fake laugh.

She was reading the Style page of the newspaper. "You should be in that section, Mom," I said. "You have good style."

She looked surprised. "Thank you, Adam," she said. "I never knew you noticed."

Being nice on purpose felt crummy because there was a good chance that she would be mad at me soon.

I was turning into a liar before my own eyes. "I think I hear the dryer buzzing," I said.

"You do?" she said. "I haven't turned it on today."

"Maybe Dad did," I said.

"I'd better check," she said.

My mom can't stand wasted buzzing. That's why I said it.

After she left, I grabbed the Frankenberry box by its gnawed corner and stuffed it in my backpack.

"The dryer wasn't buzzing," she said.

"I'm probably suffering from ringing in my ears," I said. "They have ads for it on TV."

"You'd better scoot if you're going to walk with Jonique, Lucy Rose, and Sam," she said.

When I met them in front of Congress Market I pulled the waxed-paper sack out of the box. "I lost our mouse. It found our cereal. Now I have a backpack full of Frankenberries."

"At least we have a snack," Sam said.

"That is disgusting in the absolute extreme," Lucy Rose said. "Also wretched."

"Totally," Jonique said. "I never eat anything that has had rodent feet walking on it."

"They're small feet," I said.

Jonique turned my backpack upside down and dumped everything in the market's trash can.

"Now my homework has coffee on it," I said.

I wiped it off on Jonique's red jacket. It hardly shows but now she says she's not talking to me.

20

MY NEW FRIEND, MELVIN

At school I kept wondering about home. What if my mom was making a horrible discovery right that minute? My mind was so full of that problem I didn't hear Mr. Santalices call on me until he was in front of my desk.

"We don't have anything new," I said.

"That surprises me, Adam," he said.

"Me too," I told him.

"You and Sam have less than a week to build a winning entry," he said. "Get a move on."

When the bell rang I told Sam, "We're ruined."

"At least you don't have to get your teeth checked today," he said. "I do. By Dr. Bowers."

I walked home the long way so I could think. I should have taken the even longer way.

The first alarming thing was my mom. She was standing on the white sofa, with shoes, breathing ninety miles an hour. The second thing was when she said, "Jump on the couch, Adam!"

"I'm not even allowed to sit on that couch," I said.

Her voice was squeaking. "It's an emergency!"

"What's the matter?" I said.

"Up, up, up!" she said, pulling my arm.

She let go when the phone rang.

"Mr. Thompson!" she said. "I am a desperate woman."

I'd never heard of Mr. Thompson before.

"Noises!" she said. "In my closet. They sounded like *scritch-scritch*. Then they stopped. But when I came downstairs to call my husband, the noises were inside the kitchen wall. Mr. Thompson, I know a woman who had a RACCOON in the ATTIC. She said it scritched. I probably have a whole FAMILY of raccoons."

She was quiet for a second. Then she wasn't. "I

have a CHILD here," she said. "What if these raccoons have RABIES? You have to come!"

I could hear Mr. Thompson saying something but my mom interrupted. "I can't wait until Wednesday! We're under attack. Raccoons tore HOLES in my friend's footstool. They PEED on the attic floor."

The whole time my mom was talking, she was marching up and down the sofa cushions. "Of COURSE I'll pay the emergency charge," she said. "This IS an emergency."

I felt really bad.

"Hurry," my mom told Mr. Thompson. "For all I know it's a COYOTE."

It was no use telling her that there are no coyotes on Capitol Hill. There would have been use in telling her that there was a mouse in the house, but even though I was soaking in guilt, I could not get myself to do that.

Mr. Thompson's trapping man got to us two hours and eleven minutes later. "I'll open the door," I said to my mom. "You stay on the Island of Safety." That was our new name for the sofa.

The trapping man's hair was short in the front and long in the back. He had huge leather gloves hanging off one side of his belt and the biggest ring of keys you ever saw on the other. He had a sack of little cages. One cage was big enough for a raccoon but too small for a coyote. His shirt said Melvin. I decided that if inventing doesn't work out, and it is looking like it might not, trapping could be the job for me.

My mom said, "Melvin, my son and I will be staying on the sofa until you catch it."

"Fine with me," he said. "I'll bait the kitchen first. Chances are it's a mouse."

"It can't be," my mom said, and fanned herself with her hands. "This house is clean."

"You wouldn't be the first clean house to get mice," he called out from the kitchen.

"What do you mean MICE?" my mom yelled. "You said mouse. ONE mouse."

Melvin poked his head out of the swinging door

and said, "It's rare to get just one. But don't worry, we'll catch all of them in the next few weeks."

"Weeks?" my mom croaked. "I could die of fear and embarrassment in that time. The M.O.T.H.s will think we're slobs."

"You've got moths too?"

"Not bugs, moms," she said. "Moms On The Hill."

"Okay, then," Melvin said. "Can your boy show me upstairs?"

"No!" my mom said. "He could get bitten."

"I'll be fine," I said. "I'll follow Melvin around and study his trapping ways."

I helped him take my mom's plastic shoe houses out of her closet. Then I asked him for mouse-catching tips.

"I don't go for glue traps," Melvin said. "Getting stuck can't be fun for the mice."

He put a little cage on the upstairs bathroom floor. "Mice love peanut butter," he said.

He let me put a glob in the cage that we put in my room, which he called a disaster area. When we went back down, I got to set up the mudroom trap.

Melvin was telling me about the time he and a guy named Dwayne caught a black bear in a lady's yard in West Virginia, when we heard a snap in the kitchen.

"Come to Papa," Melvin said. That's the trapper way of saying: Welcome to my trap.

I followed him through the swinging door.

"You want to tell me about this mouse?" he asked me.

I slid across the floor and knelt down by the cage.

"It's mine," I said. "I got it from a pet supply shop."

"I know that," Melvin said.

"How?" I said, sticking my hand through the wire door to massage its mouse head.

"House mice are brown," he said. "Store-bought mice are white."

"How about that!" I said.

"Did you lose more than one?" he said.

"Nope," I told him. "Just this guy."

"Good," he said. "I'll give him to a pet store."

I gave our mouse one last back tickle and helped Melvin reload the cages in his van. At least this way it wouldn't get eaten.

"By the way," I asked. "What's the best way to catch a snake?"

"In nature or in a house?" Melvin said.

"A house," I told him.

"Boy, you sure have been keeping a lot from your momma," he said.

"I know," I said.

"That's not good," he said.

"I feel rotten about it," I said. "I've lied all over the place."

"I'm not going to tell on you," Melvin said. "I believe you're going to do the honest thing."

We had a silent time. Then Melvin said, "Can take a while to locate a snake. Snake's more likely to locate you. Best I can tell you is they like damp spaces and dark places."

"Thanks," I said.

While my mom was paying, Melvin told her, "Don't worry, ma'am. This mouse was a lone traveler. You won't see another."

My mom acted like that was the most thrilling news she'd ever heard.

Dad took us to White Tiger for dinner because my mom couldn't look at our kitchen knowing a mouse had been roaming. I tried not to think about the rest of the problem that was slithering at home.

21

HUMBLE PIE

Mrs. Washburn told us to write about the most difficult time of our lives. Most kids wrote about their past. I wrote about my horrible present.

She praised Lucy Rose's story about when her parents got separated. She loved Sam's about how his parents' car broke on the drive to the hospital and his mom could have had baby Julia in a taxi. When I read mine, Mrs. Washburn said, "When you know how your story ends you'll have to tell us."

Ashley said, "I am never coming to your house."

I wanted to say "Good, because I'm never inviting you." But I didn't. These days I am staying away from extra problems.

Mr. Santalices came in the afternoon. "This is the last day for troubleshooting," he said. "The next time we meet, we will present our reinventions."

"I need my troubles shot," Lucy Rose said. "No matter what I invent, that puny dog escapes."

The class was out of ideas.

Sam said, "I solved the problem of tardiness by inventing Breakfast Bombs."

That news shocked me and made me mad. "We're a team!" I said.

Sam's face looked guilty. "I'm sorry," he said. "But we've had flop after flop. I don't want to lose."

"There are already about three hundred bars you can eat for breakfast," Bart said.

"Remember Mr. Santalices said food is not a good reinvention," Ashley said. She looked smirky.

"Bombs are," Sam said. "I mixed up ketchup, scrambled eggs, chopped bacon, orange juice, and blueberries and patted them into balls. Then I rolled them in grape jelly and granola. My motto is: Delicious, Nutritious, and Portable."

Everyone had an invention but me and maybe Ashley.

The only thing that could make my life worse happened after school. Sam said he was sorry about dropping out of our team, so I was mostly over being mad and, since I needed good ideas, I walked to Baking Divas with him and Lucy Rose and Jonique.

"You have a lot to worry about, Scout," Sam said.

"Biggest problem?" Lucy Rose asked.

"Something made me decide I had to tell my mom on myself," I said. "But how?"

"Blurt it out!" Jonique said. "You can't let your mom find a snake in the washing machine."

"That would do her in on the very spot," Lucy Rose said.

"How about saying, 'By the way, Mom, there's a chance you might see a snake in our house,'" Sam said.

" 'By the way' is good," I said. "It sounds like there's nothing to worry about."

"Throw yourself on her mercy," Lucy Rose said. "Also write her a card of sorrow."

"Okay," I said. "I'm telling the minute I get home. At least I won't have to sneak around snake hunting anymore."

When we got to the bakery, Ashley and her mom were sitting at a front table eating Buckeye Brownies. Her mom waved her arm and said: "HEL-LO, KID-DOS!" Ashley waved one finger and didn't say anything.

We waved and Lucy Rose counted our money. "We have enough for three mini-cupcakes," she said. Since Jonique's mom is a Diva, she gets hers for free.

"I wish I could live at your house," I said.

She thought I meant for the free food but I actually meant until the snake problem was over.

Then the bell on the door clanged, which is what happens when somebody opens it.

Then I heard, "Darling boy!"

"Mom!" I said. "What are you doing HERE?"

"Buying apple crumble for dessert," she said, and gave me a tight hug. Then she told Mrs. McBee, "I do NOT know what I would have done without Adam yesterday. Even though our house is clean, a mouse got in. I thought I would die from fear but Adam took charge and helped Mr. Thompson's man catch it. It made me realize how responsible he is. Lola, I'm ashamed to tell you I have been underestimating my son's maturity."

"Your ears are hot red," Lucy Rose said to me.

"There's not another boy like him," Mrs. McBee said.

"He is my one-of-a-kind lifesaver," my mom said.

"Hi, Mrs. Melon," Ashley said in her smiley voice.

"Hello, Ashley," my mom said.

"I'm really glad you got rid of the mouse," Ashley said. "But did you catch the snake?"

"Snake?" my mom said. "We don't have a snake."

"Well, actually, yes, we do," I said. "I'm really sorry."

My mom plopped down on the window seat and stared at the floor and said nothing.

"I'm sorry in the extreme," Lucy Rose said. "Sorrier than last year when I convinced Melonhead to make a vest by cutting off the sleeves of his dress-up jacket."

"You did that?" my mom said.

"And I am utterly sorry about it," Lucy Rose said.

"Why are you sorry about the snake?" my mom asked.

"Your house would be snake free if it weren't for us," Sam said.

"Sad to say, we're nothing but a band of snake smugglers," Lucy Rose told her.

"But we never, ever thought Cobra would get out," Jonique said.

"Cobra?" my mom squealed.

"He's not one," I said, fast.

"Not at all," Lucy Rose said. "He's more like a huge worm with scales."

The skin on my mom's face turned the color of watery milk. "Believe me," I said. "I would do anything to undo this."

"He has regret galore," Lucy Rose said.

"Jonique Angelica McBee. I know you know better," Mrs. McBee said.

I took my mom's hand and pulled her outside. "We'd better call Dad," I said.

By the time we walked home, he was already there. And oh, brother, was he mad.

"Betty," he said. "I'd like to talk to Adam alone."

"Thank you," my mom said. "I'm going to lie down."

At first my dad didn't speak. That was as bad as yelling.

"You know how boys are," I said.

"I do know how boys are," my dad said. "And I know how they shouldn't be. Boys want pets but boys should not sneak pets into the house. If they do, boys should hold on to them. If the pet escapes anyway, the boy must tell his parents the WHOLE truth, RIGHT AWAY. Boys who don't are in big trouble."

"Very big?" I asked him.

"Huge," my dad said.

"I'm going to write Mom a letter that will be at least three pages long," I said. "I'm going to say that I learned some lessons."

"Do you plan on saying that you are especially sorry because you knew how much she hates snakes and you did this anyway?" he said.

"Yes," I said. "I'm apologizing for the mouse, too."

"You brought the mouse into our house?" he said.

"A snake has to eat," I said.

"Apologize for both animals," he said. "But don't mention that the mouse was the snake's dinner."

"You just said I'm supposed to tell everything," I said.

"A snake swallowing a mouse is not an image your mom wants to have floating around her mind," he said.

22

STILL MISSING

"What's the word, hummingbird?" Sam asked.

"Great news! I found snake poop in the laundry room and the basement bathroom," I said.

"Way to go, Moe!" Sam said.

"It's only a little clue," I said. "Garter snakes poop even more than baby rattlesnakes. By the time I get home, there could be poop all over the place."

"Gross," Sam said.

"There's a chance I'll find him," I said. "After I cleaned up the morning poop I checked all the wet places in our house. Then made a cave out of my dad's socks and poured water on the cellar floor. It's like a snake hotel."

"How's your mom?" Sam asked.

"Not so great," I said. "This morning she was too nervous to stay inside so she decided to work on her garden."

"That's smart. She gets calm around flowers," Sam said.

"But she was scared to get her clippers in case Cobra was in the mudroom. My dad had to look in our boots and under the glove basket and on all the shelves. He found nothing at all. But when my mom took a flowerpot off the top shelf, an extension cord fell on her head and she screamed, 'There's a snake in my hair!'"

"That's hilarious," Sam said.

"Not if you saw her," I said. "When I was pouring Apple Jacks in my coat pocket, my plastic centipede fell out of the other pocket. She jumped. She thinks everything is a snake."

"Did you have to throw away a perfectly good centipede?" Sam asked.

"Yes," I said. "Then my dad gave me another talk about how everybody is scared of something and how we have to respect that."

At school Sam and I went to Mr. S for help.

"I don't know how to catch a snake," he told us. "Did you research it?"

"I searched and re-searched," I said. "One hundred times."

"Good luck, Adam," he said. "Remember, reinventions are due tomorrow and I'm counting on you."

That made my stomach flip over. "My mom's disappointed, my dad's disappointed, and now Mr. Santalices is disappointed," I told Sam.

"They'll get over it," he said.

"I know," I said. "But I'm disappointed too. Everything was great. Then it all went wrong and got worse. It's my fault. I'll never get to go to Chantilly."

"I'll help you think of a fast invention," Sam said.

"It's too late," I said. "I'm doomed."

All I wanted was to call my mom and tell her I was sick so I could go home. I didn't because I was pretty sure she needed a break from me. So I sat at my desk all day, without recess because it was raining, and without my lunch because I forgot it. The lunch aide wouldn't let me go to my locker and get my Apple Jacks. I had to eat school lunch of watery turkey and orange cheese and fruit cocktail. It was the only good thing about my day.

After school, Lucy Rose tried to cheer me up. "Jonique and I will walk you home," she said. "Out of pity for your terrible life."

"Thanks," I told her.

"Do you have any cereal in your pocket?" she asked. "I'm starving to bits."

I was starting to get her some Apple Jacks when Sam said, "We can split my Sno-Balls."

The girls got the insides and we got the igloos. I was feeling so crummy I ate mine without even trying on my marshmallow beard.

At Third Street Lucy Rose said, "I'm turning off here. It's my mom's day off and we're going to see the musical of *South Pacific* at Duke Ellington High School."

"Bye," I said.

"It's one hilarious show," she said. "Probably you can come if you want, Melonhead."

"I don't," I said.

"Are you feeling nothing but gloom?" she asked.

"Nothing but," I said.

"I hope it doesn't last forever," she said.

Lucy Rose was a half block away when she started running back screaming, "Wait up, you guys."

"I'll bet she came up with a foolproof snake-trapping plan!" Sam said.

"No doubt!" Jonique said.

"Lucy Rose," I hollered. "What are you thinking?"

"That I would like some Apple Jacks," she said.

"You were my last hope," I said. "I thought your original thinking was going to save the day."

"Sorry," she said. "I didn't mean to deject you."

"You can't help it," I said, and I reached in my

pocket and scooped up some Apple Jacks for her. Then I screamed. "Holy moly! Thank you, Lucy Rose!" I almost hugged her but I punched her arm instead.

Right there in my pocket, where it had been all day long, hiding in a cave made of Apple Jacks, was Cobra.

I kissed his miniature head and we made a detour to give him a soak in the Library of Congress's birdbath. Then I dropped him back in my pocket.

"Where are you taking him?" Lucy Rose asked.

"Home," I said.

"You are an utter crackpot," she said.

Jonique rolled her eyes. "I'm going with Lucy Rose. I *do not* want to see your mother seeing that snake."

"What do you think, Sam?" I asked.

"I think by the time we get there you will have a pocket full of snake poop," he said.

We ran the whole way to my house. Then I gave Sam my coat and told him, "Stay on the sidewalk."

My mom answered and I have to say, she was looking terrible. Her shoulders were slumpy. "Hello, Adam," she said. "The snake is still on the loose."

"Your worries are over, Mom," I said. "Cobra was in my jacket pocket the whole time!"

"Are you kidding?" my mom asked.

"I would never kid you about a snake, Mom," I said.

"Where did you let it go?" she said.

"I still have it," I said.

"Oh, Adam," she said. "You cannot possibly think that snake is coming back into this house."

"I don't," I said. "But I want you to see Cobra and know I'm honest. Then your nerves can rest. After that we'll give him back to nature."

"We're having some personal responsibility," Sam yelled to her.

"I don't want to see the snake," she said.

"You can stay on the porch," I told her. "And hold my hand for comfort."

She squinched her eyelids until they were almost closed. "Okay," she said.

Sam held Cobra over his head and Cobra wiggled so my mom would know he was no fake snake.

"I'll put him away now," Sam said.

"No," my mom said. "Adam, get the camera. I want you to have a picture for your memory wall."

When I came back, my mom was on the middle step, with two steps behind her and two in front.

"Keep going," I said. "When you meet him, you'll love him."

"This is far enough," she said. "I'll take pictures of the three of you. When I'm done, I want you boys to walk as far away from this house as you are allowed to go, and give that snake his freedom."

"That's a deal, Lucille," I said.

23

DO THEY HAVE A LOSER'S BUS?

"You lucked out," my dad said.

"Did I ever," I said.

"I hope next time you'll think before you do something."

"I hope so too," I said.

"Try your best," he said.

"I always do," I told him.

My dad put his arm around me. "I know you do, Sport," he said.

"Did you know that Mom got a little near Cobra?" I asked.

"We'll have to compliment her on her bravery," he said.

I came up with so much praise that my mom's ears got red and she said, "Let's celebrate this happy ending at Gifford's ice cream parlor."

"I can't," I said. "I still have a problem to solve."

"Does it have to do with snakes or mice?" my dad asked.

"Or trees? Or roofs? Or dentists?"

"None of them," I said.

I went to my room, sat on my bed, and looked at all my reinventions that didn't work. To be scientific I wrote in the log, "Results: Nothing."

Then I lay on the floor and thought about what I could make by tomorrow. Answer: Nothing.

Since Mr. S was going to be unhappy with me, I decided to do something my mom would like. I washed the mouse evidence out of her flip-flop box and put it back in her closet. Then I put the periscope in mine. I wiped Cobra's aquarium and put the empty peanut butter and jelly bowl in the dishwasher. I shoved my shoes in the closet. I picked Silly Putty out of my rug, stuffed my dirty clothes under my bed, and threw away the jar of fake blood that I made from dye and Karo syrup. Underneath was a very old snack that used to be a fish stick, I think. Chucking it was a sad job because it had hairy green mold growing on it. I kept thinking, "What if Alexander Fleming threw his mold away?" He wouldn't have discovered penicillin, that's what. That mold turned out to be a lifesaver.

Maybe it was because my room was so clean but all of a sudden I had a complete brain flash. "Dad!" I screamed. "I wasn't looking at the big picture!"

"Now you are?" he asked.

"I am," I said. "And boy, is it clear. But I will be ruined if Sam can't come over right now."

Mr. Alswang was nice but firm. "Two hours. No more. And NO CASTS."

Sam got to my house faster than ever. It took nine minutes to explain but by the time Mr. Alswang came to pick up Sam, the Rescuer was ready.

"We're going to win, Lynn," I said.

"Go to bed, Melonhead," Sam said.

I got up at five in the morning. I reinspected

everything. Then I jumped around in the shower, boxing the air and making up a song called "Res-Q-U," in case our invention ever gets advertised on TV. At 5:30, I pulled my Red Hot Fireballs soccer T-shirt over my head and put on my jeans while I went down the steps. That wasn't the best time-saver since I had to stop and put ice on my elbows after I tripped. To make up for the lost minutes I cooked toast while I put on my socks. Then I smeared butter on it with my fin-

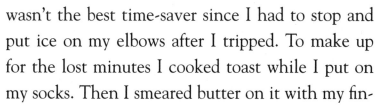

gers. To show I was still sorry, I put the toast on a glass plate and carried it upstairs. "It's like room service," I told my parents.

We only get that when we are visiting in Florida. "You are my darling boy," my mom said.

I don't mind when she says that when we're in private.

Sam's mom drove us to school. We rode in the back with Julia because that's the law, but the Rescuer was buckled up in the front. "It's the safest way," Sam said.

"Don't worry," his mom said. "I'll use care."

"You scare," Julia said, and pointed at Sam.

"I am not," Sam said.

I was a little scared but I didn't admit it.

When we got to the classroom Mr. S and Mrs. Timony were waiting. Everybody except Robinson and Ashley set up their reinventions. "My dad is bringing mine," Ashley said.

"Mr. Santalices, can I go first?" I shouted.

He picked Robinson.

She stood in front of the room and said, "My reinvention is called Handy Candy."

Then she had a coughing attack and had to cover her mouth. "Excuse me," she said.

"Can you continue?" Mr. Santalices asked.

"That was my demonstration," Robinson said.

"Handy Candy is for when you are in school or any place where you're not allowed to take a sugar break."

Then she pulled her sweatshirt over her head so it was inside out. "See these two pieces of green hose going up my sleeves?" she asked. "They are full of Twizzlers. Whenever I'm in the mood for sugar, I shake one arm and candy slides down and I catch it in my hand. Then I fake-cough. When my hand is over my mouth, I take a bite. Then I raise my hand so the Twizzler that's left slides back up to my armpit for later."

"That is one of the most supreme ideas of the century!" I said.

"I've been testing it for two weeks," she said. "I never got caught."

"Brilliant!" Mr. Santalices said.

"The next time you cough I'll pay close attention," Mrs. Timony said.

Lucy Rose went next. "This is my reinvention," she said.

"That is a wooden spoon," Ashley said.

"It used to be a spoon," Lucy Rose said. "Now it's a Puppy Stopper. I tried seven or eleven things to keep Rex from getting through the fence. Nothing worked until I took Madam's cooking spoon and tied it to her neck. Not Madam's neck. The dog's neck. Actually, her collar. Now Rex can poke her head through the fence but her body is stuck in the yard."

"Can the dog's head get stuck?" Mr. S asked.

"No, because it's only for teensy-headed dogs. Big and medium dogs stay in the yard automatically."

"What made you think of the Puppy Stopper?" Mr. S asked.

"I was desperate like you can't believe and suddenly in a snap, this brilliantine reinvention appeared in my mind," Lucy Rose said. "The only trouble with it was that people kept knocking on Madam and Pop's door and telling them, 'Your dog has a spoon on his neck.' So I glittered it up and added purple ribbons that came for free with my mom's perfume. Now it is a dog decoration and a Puppy Stopper."

"That works," Mr. Santalices said.

"I reinvented my mom earrings out of something nobody wants," Marco said.

Mrs. Timony was the earring model. They hung down as long as her hair and looked like knots. I am not a beauty judge but I'd say those earrings have zero percent attraction.

"Most unusual," Mr. Santalices said. "What did you recycle to make these works of art?"

"Chicken bones," Marco said.

"No way," Pierra said. "They're carved wood."

"Wrong," Marco said. "I soaked the bones in acetic acid for three weeks. They turned so soft I could tie a knot in them."

"Not fair," Sam said. "He got to use real acid!"

Mr. S smiled. "Tell us which acid you used."

"It's called $HC_2H_3O_2$," Marco said. "But you can also call it vinegar."

"Since when can vinegar do that?" I said.

"Since forever," he said. "Vinegar dissolves calcium, which is what bones are full of."

"How come they're hard now?" Marisol asked.

"Once they were knotted, I cooked them in the oven. That hardened them up again but since most of the calcium was sucked out the earrings can break easily. The same thing happens to people bones if they don't have enough milk and calcium foods."

"Great job," Mr. Santalices said.

Then he called on Sam.

"Melonhead and I did it together after all," Sam said.

"I'm glad," Mr. S said. "I was afraid Adam had given up."

"I never give up," I said, and I put my arms through the straps we cut off my last-year backpack.

Sam and I walked to the front of the class and he announced, "Presenting: the Rescuer."

Mr. S told the class, "That's enough laughing."

"People probably laughed at the Jaws of Life in the beginning," I whispered to Sam.

"Are you caught in a situation?" Sam said in his TV announcer voice. "No problem. The Rescuer will rescue you."

I turned around so everyone could see my back and Sam said, "These four long, flexible, tan tubes are SUPPLY TANKS."

"They're your mother's panty hose," Bart screamed. Then he laughed so hard he made donkey noises.

Sam ignored him. "The supply tanks contain Sno-Balls, cereal, a bandana, peanut butter, Gummi Worms, Breakfast Bombs, water, scissors, and bread."

"Also rope, string, a dollar, plaster of Paris cloth, a chandelier crystal, duct tape, a candle, used balloons, and diapers," I said.

"Saved by diapers!" Amir laughed.

Sam took out the crystal. "Let's say you're surrounded by wild cheetahs," he said. "Swing this back and forth so they get hypnotized. Or, at least, so dazzled by rainbows that they forget about making you into dinner."

"Thanks to Marco, we know how to turn sunshine and this ordinary crystal into a smoke machine," I said. "Smoke will make a lot of animals vamoose. Then you make a fire to light the candle so you can see when it gets dark."

Sam took out duct tape and my collection of flattened silver balloons.

"Is that in case you have an emergency birthday party?" Josh asked.

"No," I said. "If you are stranded on a desert island, lay the flat balloons on the sand in the shape of SOS to send a reflecting message to planes flying over you."

"Or if you are in a forest, being stalked by a wild boar, hold up the balloons like mirrors so the boar will think it's being attacked by a pack of boars and run away," Sam said.

"The balloons are also foldable buckets," I explained. "Whenever you see a waterfall, fill them up, tie them shut,

and put them in an expanding supply tank until you're thirsty."

I pushed half of one balloon inside the other half and put it on like a hat. "If you're freezing in Alaska, you will find out fast that thirty percent of your body heat escapes through your head," I said. "Unless you are wearing a heat-holding Mylar hat."

Even Lucy Rose and Jonique laughed.

"I don't care about looking like a nut," I said. "Men wear whatever will keep them safe."

Sam held up the duct tape. "This tape is a bad way to keep a pacifier in a baby but good for practically everything else."

"If you tape the balloons together, you've got a blanket," I said.

"And if you are getting soaked in the rain forest, the blanket turns into a waterproof roof."

"If the storm blew off your clothes and you're naked, just duct-tape banana leaves together and make a kilt," Sam said. "Pants are harder."

"To get off an island, all you have to do is find bamboo, tape it together, and presto! You have a raft," I said. "And if you must trap a small, fierce animal that would otherwise eat you alive, wrap tape around a tree so the sticky side is out like a glue trap. Press some of the cereal on it and, the next thing you know, the animal is caught and you're safe."

"If you break your arm, you can support it with a stick and duct tape," Sam said. "And when the swelling goes down you can make a professional cast."

I showed our leftover plaster-soaked gauze and said, "Warning: Do NOT use for fun."

Sam held up his sawed-in-half cast. "To make an emergency cast, take a balloon full of water and pour it on the plaster cloth and wrap the patient's arm."

"But you don't have to break a bone to use it," I said. "You can blow up a balloon and wrap wet gauze around half of it. In about fifteen minutes you'll have a cereal bowl that's also a cup," Sam said. "To make it waterproof, just make a fire, light the candle, and drip wax all over the inside."

"We know what the food is for," Bart said.

"To eat, of course," I said, and made a distraction of myself by eating a Breakfast Bomb. I didn't mention that it needed more ketchup.

Then Sam spun around wearing a pink goatee. "If you are spying on someone, Sno-Balls make a good disguise," he said. "Also a delicious meal for a person, or if you are cornered by savage animals, a delicious meal for them."

"Why are you wearing coat hangers for a belt?" Hannah asked, nicely.

Sam did a demonstration. "So we'd have hooks to hang our periscope and this sound magnifier."

I got that idea from Gus.

"That sound magnifier looks like an umbrella," Marco said.

"It is good for rain-storms and sun protec-tion," I said. "But it's also for scaring bad guys."

"I'm sure bad guys are terrified of umbrellas," Ashley said.

Sam opened the magnifier while I pulled the elbows off our periscope. Then I aimed the plastic pipe at the inside of the umbrella and barked.

"You do sound scary," Clayton said.

"That's because the sound waves go through the tube and bounce off the umbrella," Sam said. "That makes them come back louder."

"That's not all hangers are good for," I said, taking one off my waist. "If you are chased to a cliff with no escape ahead but

there are vines growing from one side to the other, just hook a hanger around a vine. And presto, you have a zip line to slide across the ravine."

"We didn't get to test this," Sam said, "because we didn't have a ravine."

"Don't lose the hanger when you get to the other side," I said. "It will save you again if you get captured and held prisoner in a creepy jail. You can unbend it and pick the lock. But don't undo the curved part, because if the keys are on a guard's belt, you can wait until he is asleep. The wire will give almost forty inches of extra arm. Just hook the keys and let yourself out."

"And if you are starving on a boat, put a Gummi Worm on the hanger hook and pull in a fish," Sam said. "Then use the hanger to hold the fish over the fire."

"Why don't you put all this stuff in a backpack instead of embarrassing panty hose?" Josh asked.

"A backpack won't shield your body," I said.

Then Sam cut a hole in the middle of one pair of our tanks. "If you are in a swamp full of mosquitoes and don't want to get the awful disease of malaria, put your head through the hole and your arms in the legs. Then pull the elastic down over your shirt like you are putting on a sweater," he said. "Pull the other pair over your shorts and use Total Body Protection."

"They smell," Marisol said. "Like my grandma."

"The body shields have been improved and fortified by a soak in lavender oil," I said. "Mosquitoes despise lavender."

"You forgot the wrapping-paper tube that's for getting away from the carbon dioxide," Pierra said.

"We don't need it," Sam said. "We breathe through the periscope pipe."

"The periscope also helps us see what's going on above us," I said. "Also, the mirror that's inside comes out when we need to flash SOS signals."

"Big deal," Ashley said. "How many times is a person stuck in a swamp in Alaska filled with mosquitoes and cheetahs?"

"I hope I am at least once in my life," I said. "Anyway, supply tanks do more than keep away mosquitoes."

Sam yanked off his panty hose shirt and gave it to me. Then he peeled off his panty hose pants. We each held them up by a foot and tied the legs together by making a knot every twelve inches. "Does anyone need a ladder?" I asked.

"That will not hold a person," Kathleen said.

"It will," Sam said. "Nylon is strong."

"If, for some reason, you are on a roof and need a quick way down, you tie it to something and climb down," I said.

"Also since they are not airtight you can use supply tubes to carry around snakes or bugs you want to keep," I said.

"What's the dollar for?" Robinson asked.

"My mom says you shouldn't travel without money," Sam said.

"What about the diapers?" Bart asked.

"They are the best part," Sam said.

Everybody laughed but this time I didn't mind. I took off my shoe and said, "Let's say your foot gets stuck in a hole in a tree and you can't get it out."

"Okay," Mr. Santalices said. "Let's say that happened."

"When your foot is stuck like that it sweats like crazy," I said. "But the sweat just soaks the foam in the bottom of your shoe and makes it even tighter."

Sam cut open two diapers and poured the crystals into my new high-top sneaker. "Super-absorbent polymers are the secret ingredient in diapers. One pound of these can soak up fifty gallons of water," I said.

"Or sweat," Sam said. "And since we don't have all day to wait for Melonhead to sweat, I poured half a bottle of water in his new shoe."

Then I put on my shoe. "One thing I learned is DO NOT tie your shoes with double knots."

While we waited for it to work, Sam cut open three more diapers, and poured the crystals into the yellow bandana we borrowed from Lucy Rose.

"I'm rolling it up and soaking it in water," Sam said. Then he tied it around his neck. "If you are roasting in a desert the Instant Refresher will keep your neck wet for hours."

"Now we need some volunteers," I said.

We picked Amir and Jonique and gave them the job of holding my shoe to the floor while I pulled my leg. After a few minutes my foot oozed out.

"P-U," Jonique said.

"D-double D-sgusting," Lucy Rose said.

"Awesome," Bart said.

"Thank you," I told him.

"Why does that work?" Mr. Santalices said.

"The slippery polymer mush expands around my foot so it's a lot easier to pull out," I said.

"What if you don't get stuck in a tree and you're left with a shoe full of diaper jelly?" Clayton said.

"Then you just have the fun of it," I said.

"The end," Sam said.

And the whole class started clapping and stamping their feet and yelling. Marisol said, "Fantastic!"

Hannah called out, "Brilliant!"

Mr. Santalices said, "Did you write this down in your log?"

I showed him our book. He read it out loud. "Results: Lots of wrongs equals one right."

"That is the nature of inventing," Mr. S said. "And your reinvention is a superior one."

"I never felt so good in my life," I told Sam.

"Same with me," he said.

"We're stars, Lars," I said.

24
BEST IN SHOW

Ashley's dad came after lunch. He put a rectangle covered with a tablecloth in front of Mrs. Timony's desk. Sticking out of the bottom was an electric plug. When Ashley put it in the socket and pulled off the cloth the whole class sucked in their breath. "This is a lie detector," Ashley said.

There were red and green Christmas lights and next to them letters that said True and Lie. "I wish I could do letters like that," Hannah said. "They're perfect."

Over the lightbulbs was a thing that looked like the speedometer in my dad's car.

"I wish my Dusting Wand display looked like that," Kathleen said.

Ashley smiled at her. "Who wants to try it?"

Everybody raised their hands.

"I pick Marisol," Ashley said.

Marisol ran to the front.

Ashley gave her two things that looked like jump rope handles only they were made of metal. "Hold one of these in each hand," Ashley said.

Marisol squeezed them.

"Say your name," Ashley told her.

"Marisol Fernandez," Marisol said.

The green light went on and everybody clapped.

Then Ashley put her face near Marisol's and gave her a scary stare. "Do you have any secrets?"

"No," Marisol said.

The red light lit up.

"Are you sure about that?" Ashley said.

"Thank you for the demonstration, Marisol," Mr. Santalices said. "You may go back to your seat."

"I'm not done," Ashley said.

"From now on, you can test me," Mr. Santalices said. "But first, tell us how this machine works."

"It's got wires on the back," Ashley said.

"What do they do?" he asked her.

"Connect to the lightbulbs and that dial," she said.

"How does it know when you're lying?" Amir said.

"It just does," Ashley said.

"Remember, Ash," her dad said, "the detector measures if the person's hands are sweating."

"Right," Ashley said. "Because liars sweat."

"What are the recycled parts?" Pierra asked.

Ashley looked at her dad. "Christmas tree lights," she said.

"And the dial," her dad said.

"The dial," Ashley said.

Mrs. Timony pointed to the clock. "One minute until the bell," she said. "Pack up your entries and take them to the gym."

"I admit it," I told Sam. "That is the reinvention of all time."

"Maybe we'll come in second," he said.

25
HOO BOY!

This was the great day of all days. My dad went to the office late so he could come with Mom and me to the Challenge America! assembly in the lunchroom.

I almost couldn't stay in my folding chair. First the principal gave a speech about being proud of us. Mr. Santalices told us that our reinventions showed creative thinking and told the parents to look out because some of their kids might be the Alexander Graham Bells of tomorrow. I whispered to my dad, "I hope not because the telephone has already been invented."

Finally Mr. S said we could get up and look at

the displays. "Wait until you see Ashley's," I told my mom.

"I'm eager to try it out," my mom said. "You've been talking about it since yesterday."

"She's going to win," Josh said.

A lot of moms thought Ted Meany's face-wrinkle removers were the best thing in the fifth-grade aisle. They looked like Band-Aids only the white square on the sticky side was green.

"Avocado is good for skin," Ted said. "So I tried taping clumps of it on my mom's face. They wouldn't stay stuck. Then I tried guacamole on her but it slid off. Next I rubbed avocado pieces on Band-Aids. Then I put lemon juice on top of that so the avocado wouldn't turn brown."

"That's because lemon juice is an acid," I told my mom.

"Let me know if you go into business, Ted," she said. "I'll buy a box."

My dad told my mom, "You have the skin of a twenty-year-old."

"Then you'd better give it back," I said. That got everybody laughing.

We only got to see Ashley's for a second. My mom said she couldn't believe it and my dad agreed.

"Please come back at three o'clock to see which of these fine reinventions take the prizes," Mr. S said.

"I can't wait that long," I said.

"See you at three, darling boy," my mom said.

"Call me if you win, Sport," my dad said. "Or if you don't."

All we did after that was go to school all afternoon and try to spy on the judges at recess. Right when I thought I'd explode, BAM! It was time. My mom was waiting in the gym with Sam's parents. Before we could even find the Rescuer we heard a girl screaming, "I won!" It was Lucy Rose.

I like my friends to win things but I did not like her to win this thing. "No offense but her reinvention is nothing but a painted spoon," I told my mom.

We found Lucy Rose. Her mom and Madam and Pop were taking a picture of her holding the Puppy Stopper. Her mom looked like she would pop from happiness. "Want to see my ribbon?" Lucy Rose asked.

It was yellow and beautiful. "Great job," I told her.

"I won for Least Expensive to Make!" she said.

"Really great," I said. This time I meant it.

We passed Jonique's Personal Moving Bath Mats that are made of two sponges glued to two pot holders and ribbons. "You tie one to each foot and they dry while you walk and the sponges mop up the drips," she said.

My mom, Mrs. Alswang and Julia, and Sam and I got all the way down the aisle but didn't find the Rescuer. "Wait one second here," I said. "The next aisle is for the third graders' reinventions."

"I can't believe the Rescuer is not on display," Sam said. "Where's Mr. Santalices?"

We started to look for him but then we interrupted ourselves. "There's the Rescuer!" I shouted. "Onstage!"

"With a blue ribbon!" Sam said.

"Mom!" I shouted. "It says Best in Show!"

She called my dad and he taxied over. Sam and I

took turns wearing the Rescuer while his dad took pictures. Then the lady from the *Hill Rag* newspaper took some. "This is a scoop," I told her.

"Indeed it is," she said.

We had a double family celebration at Las Placitas. I got tacos and Sprite and fried ice cream for dessert. And when the owner heard that we won he said, "It's an honor to have you in my restaurant," and gave us chips and salsa for free.

"I can't believe Ashley's didn't win anything," Sam said.

"Me either," I said.

"Mr. Santalices said she decided not to enter," Sam's mom said.

"I will never figure out what goes on in the heads of girls," I said.

Sam's dad said, "I like what's going on in the heads of you boys."

"Hoo boys!" Julia said.

My dad held up his Diet Coke and said, "I am so proud of you."

"Loud of yoooo," Julia said.

"I'm tickled pink," my mom said.

"Pickled tink," Julia said.

Sam and I high-fived with both hands.

"We're going to Chantilly, silly," I said.

ABOUT THE AUTHOR

Like Melonhead, Katy Kelly grew up in Washington, D.C., on Capitol Hill, five blocks away from the Capitol of the United States. Unlike Melonhead, she does not enjoy rodents, taking shortcuts across her neighbors' roofs, or exploding things. But they both love adventures, have sweet teeth for all desserts, and have a hilarious friend named Lucy Rose. Katy Kelly lives in Washington, D.C., with her artist husband and their fabulous daughters, Emily and Marguerite. This is her fifth book for young readers and her first in the Melonhead series.

ABOUT THE ILLUSTRATOR

Gillian Johnson and her family lived for ten years in Tasmania, Australia, a place far from Capitol Hill, where all the snakes are extremely poisonous. To avoid any Melonhead-like mishaps, her family opted for a nonpoisonous, blue-tongued pet lizard they called Bluey.

Gillian Johnson is a UK-based author/illustrator who lives in Oxford with her husband and two sons.

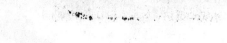